DOOMFRYS CASTLE

Sarah Fenton Collins

Wallpaper Novella Publishing
California

This book is a work of fiction. Names, characters, places, and incidents are either products of the author's imagination or used fictitiously. Any resemblance to actual events or locales, or persons, living or dead, is entirely coincidental.

For information regarding special discounts for bulk purchases, please contact Wallpaper Novella Publishing at:
wallpapernovellapublishing@gmail.com

Cover Design by S.F. Collins, Lara Edmanson, and Danja Collins
Interior sketch by Lara Edmanson

Library of Congress Cataloging-in-Publication Data
Names: Collins, Sarah Fenton, author
Title: Doomfrys Castle/ By Sarah Fenton Collins
Description: Sunnyvale, CA: Wallpaper Novella Publishing, 2025
Identifiers: LCCN 2025919840 (print)
ISBN 978196332005 (pbk.) | 9781969332012 (digital)

ISBN: 978-1-969332-00-5

Manufactured in the United States of America

Dedication

Whether in the Wasatch Mountains or along the shores of Lake Powell, my siblings and I grew up listening to this story from our dad, a master storyteller. As teens, we shared it with friends around the campfire after long days of water skiing. At dusk, we'd beg, "Tell *Doomfrys*, Dad!" He'd protest, "You've all heard it!" but always relented with a familiar twinkle in his eye. Now, our children gather in a circle to hear Grandpa tell it, waiting for the infamous jump scare that never fails to send first-timers flying.

My father first heard a version of this tale from his scout leader in the late 1950s or early 1960s. Over the years, he adapted it, always in first person, shaping the story to fit the setting, adding lines like "and then the wind began to blow, just like now," as a breeze swept through camp. To us, the main character was always Dad himself, brave, calm, and steady.

Of course, my dad's thirty-minute campfire yarn wasn't a full novel. But through family brainstorming and shared memories, it grew. What began as a gift to preserve our father's legacy became a tale that felt too vivid not to share.

It's always been *Doomfrys Castle* ("doom-frees"), with the name itself a hint of what was to come. However, while researching for this short novel, I discovered that Dumfries, Scotland, has a historic castle and has ties to early settlers in Dumfries, Virginia, in the 1600s. The coincidence offered rich inspiration, but we couldn't part with the ominous feel of *Doomfrys*. Though loosely inspired by real places and events, this story is entirely a work of fiction.

Any shortcomings in this tale are mine alone and in no way reflect my father, whose brilliant storytelling has captivated generations around the firelight with his blend of suspense and delight. *Doomfrys Castle* is a story we now share with you, but at its heart, it is a tribute to our father.

For you, Dad.
With love,
~Sarah

PART ONE

I.

A Scottish Chieftain raised two sons. One would fight to uphold the clan's honor; the other would nearly bring it to ruin.

The day the first son was born, the midwife ran from the mother's room, exclaiming, *"The clan is blessed! A male heir has been born!"* The Chieftain hugged the midwife and proclaimed that this special child would be named for him and his fathers before him. His namesake, Colyne, would one day lead the clan.

Great relief washed over the clan, knowing that the future was secure, and the village of Doomfrys rejoiced.

Four years later, a second male child was born. It was heralded that the house was now twice blessed with sons. Ihon, with his light blond curls and witty eyes, bore a striking resemblance to his mother, Mavis. It was no secret that Mavis favored her younger child. She held him in her arms continually, most of her attention given to his joyful smiles or his wailing cries.

Groomed from birth to lead, Colyne spent much of his youth at his father's side, learning of grit, decisiveness, and justice. As a very small child, he rode tucked in the saddle, in front of the great Chieftain, his father, clutching the reins of a towering black stallion as they traveled from village to village, calling on their kinsmen. Farmers bowed low to show their respect, mothers offered fresh bread from their hot ovens, and the people listened with reverence and powerful loyalty.

Colyne bore witness to the fellowship among them. The Chieftain listened before speaking, but once his decisions were made, he acted swiftly, a hard man, but a fair landlord. The customs were kept, the harvests tithed, but never more than a family could bear. The Chieftain saw to it that every table was well stocked, and even a few luxuries found their way into the homes. It was around the feast fire of farmers and clansmen that Colyne came to understand the weight of responsibility upon his father's shoulders.

Ihon, in turn, quickly grew possessive of his mother's attention. He ignored corrections from anyone else and relished in the mischief he could slip past, knowing she would answer only with a softened rebuke, often softened further by the spark of pride, a gleam of humor, in her eyes at his cleverness. She excused this indulgence for Ihon by reminding herself that Colyne would inherit everything; why shouldn't Ihon claim the lion's share of *her* love? She was proud of her eldest, but knew he would never truly belong to her.

Colyne, pure of heart, understood this. He did not begrudge his young brother this affection but rather focused on learning from his father.

The years passed, and the brothers grew older and taller. Both young men bore the unmistakable look of their clan, easily recognized as Chieftain Doomfrys' sons. Colyne's broad shoulders and strong jaw commanded instant recognition; his steady presence brought comfort in the future. But Ihon's taciturn intensity and his piercing stare unsettled all who met his gaze.

The long, bitter winter of Ihon's thirteenth year brought more than snow to the lowlands; it carried chill and sickness on the wind, sweeping across all of Scotland. Frost clung to the thatched rooftops without melting, and the rivers froze solid from bank to bank. Game grew scarce on the moors and within a day's ride of the castle.

Word spread amongst the glen and villages that animals were dying, and children and parents alike were burning up with sickness.

Even the halls of Doomfrys Castle were not spared. While her boys played robustly in quarantined solitude, their mother, Mavis, took ill. Her forehead burned with fire, and her body trembled with chills. In her heart, she knew she had little time left.

Mavis called Ihon to her bedside, *"Please read,"* she asked, and Ihon did. With only pages left in her Book of Sonnets, she took Ihon's hand in hers and told him of her love for him, confirming yet again that he was her favored one.

The months passed, and her body slowly withered away. Eventually, the fight left her completely. Too weak to explain to Ihon, she whispered to *"fetch warm tea."* Ihon resisted, but she insisted, *"Go, my son. Fetch it."*

Ihon's chest tightened with panic he didn't understand. He ran to the castle kitchen, desperate to return to his mother's side as quickly as possible.

Before he could return, a painful cry rang out from the castle walls above. "Chieftain, hurry, she is going!" the maid shouted.

Ihon dropped the tray he carried and sprinted back. But Mavis, Lady of the castle and clan, was already gone. In her chambers, the Chieftain cradled her limp body tight to his chest. Colyne stood nearby.

"She's gone, my sons" his father said, voice breaking in agony. "Your mother is gone."

Ihon's eyes burned as he looked upon his mother in the arms of his father. Jealousy and fury seethed within him. Rage that she had sent him away, jealousy that it wasn't him to be her companion in death. She *loved him*, not his father. His chest heaved, choking back cries. Betrayal! The last moments of his mother were given to the almighty Chieftain and his self-righteous heir. Did they not already possess everything else?

Ihon wanted to scream and shove his father aside, push him out of the room, away from his beloved mother. He wanted everyone to leave the room. He would hold her hand until it was cold and rotting. He'd whisper to her, asking death to release her, as if life could still be persuaded.

But they wouldn't let him, he knew it. Ihon's anger brimmed and boiled upward; soon it would explode in an uncontrollable rage. His eyes turned to thin slits, and he glared across the room at his brother. He was tempted to mock the anguish on Colyne's face, *as if he knew anything of love!*

Colyne's pity, so evident, so pained, bristled Ihon further. His brother reached out to him, but Ihon wouldn't accept. He hit the proffered hand away. What did his brother know of his torture? Colyne had their father, and now Ihon had nothing but the all-consuming rage building in his chest.

So instead, Ihon ran. He ran to the darkest, most secret parts of the castle. He screamed and wailed. He shrieked and gnashed his teeth. His lips formed hateful words into rants that his voice carried where no one would hear him. He banged his fists against the stone walls. He screamed at his mother for sending him away. He blamed his father for her death, spending so much time away when Mavis lay ill. Instead, he'd been solving the ridiculous problems of peasants when he should have been looking after his mother's care.

Ihon spat on the ground at the very thought of his brother, *the favored son, the golden heir*. Colyne's face loomed before his eyes, calm and superior. *One day*, he thought, one day he would avenge his mother, and they would know of the secret of Mavis's heart, that *she had whispered silently to him through her care,* that he was the one, the clever one, the rightful one. He hated them all, and any remaining fragment of tenderness in his heart burned up in the flame of his fury.

II.

The years passed, and Colyne continued to learn from his father. The Castle Doomfrys was strategically placed to protect the River Nith and the southern borders of Scotland; therefore, Colyne took his role to protect the lowlands seriously and became versed in the governance of kin and hearth.

No amount of urging from the Chieftain would entice Ihon to join them in clan meetings, training, or hunts. Ihon refused any offering of community.

In truth, Chieftain Doomfrys felt a measure of relief at the separation. Seeing the eyes of his dead wife in his second child caused him a sharp, lingering pain. He realized too late that he had wrongly indulged his precious wife's coddling of their young son, to Ihon's lasting detriment.

Ihon felt only his father's disappointment, not understanding that it was disappointment in himself, not in his son. His father's words, though filled with cheerful affirmations and direction, were always tinged with regret and disdain. Ihon stayed away and waited.

In time, Colyne proved himself capable and steady, so his father entrusted him with the care of the castle and clan while he departed to the highlands to oversee their lands and flocks. Colyne ruled with a balanced hand, kind to the people, yet firm in his adherence to Scottish custom.

He extended what grace he could toward Ihon, reaching out as far as pride and duty would allow. But though the clan's love for him grew, so too did the quiet sorrow in his heart; for all his effort, he could not reach his brother. And Colyne longed, more than he would ever admit, for solidarity with Ihon, to have his brother at his right hand.

With the chieftain in the highlands, the brothers moved like twin planets, sharing the same sky, yet never the same orbit. Colyne flourished under the trust of the clansmen, proving himself a fair businessman and a gifted planner. At twenty-five, he would soon choose a bride, and the clan looked eagerly to the future under his leadership.

Ihon, meanwhile, withdrew deeper into the shadows. Rarely seen by the people, he wandered the castle halls and slipped through its forgotten passageways, whispering to himself thoughts of vengeance and ruin. While Colyne built a future, Ihon nursed and sharpened a grudge. Sometimes he spoke these dark musings aloud to the spirit of Mavis, and she seemed to approve. With bitter guile and a twisted heart deformed by old wounds, Ihon began to shape a plan.

III.

It was a night like any other in the great hall, the smell of roasting pork and peat smoke hanging heavy in the air, and the long wooden tables crowded with kin and clan, servants and patrons. The great hearth burned orange, and a single suckling piglet turned on the spit, the other removed and carved, resting on a platter before Colyne.

Colyne stood and held the carving knife above his head. "My clansmen, you join me in work; now let us join for nourishment. Thanks be to God for this meal."

"Thanks be to God," repeated the small crowd.

Ihon bowed his head, but did not utter the words. He approached his brother and stood awkwardly in front of him. Surprised, Colyne looked up and set the knife down.

"Brother, there is a seat here, by me," he said.

Ihon nodded and maneuvered around the table and to the empty chair. He had no desire for small talk.

"Colyne, I'm ready to learn from you. I've been stubborn, and I need work to fill my time," Ihon said abruptly, his voice low and controlled.

Colyne's eyes widened, and he blinked twice, and for a breathless moment, time stood still. Ihon shifted in his seat, the weight of the silence pressing down on him.

And then Colyne's face split into a wide grin. He rose from his chair with a rush of warmth and pulled Ihon into a fierce embrace, his strong arms wrapping around his brother's slighter frame. Ihon froze, standing stiff in his grasp. His eyes, glinting from the firelight, narrowed. His lips curled into a fleeting snarl, gone in an instant.

"I can think of no better news than this, Ihon," Colyne said, releasing Ihon from his hold. "Come, let us speak of the possibilities. I need your help to build our clan. Brother, we are stronger together."

Over the next few months, Ihon went everywhere, did everything, with Colyne. He played his part perfectly. He rode beside him through heather-covered hills and muddy town roads, flashing false smiles at strangers and kinsmen alike. He joined in trade discussions at the long oak table in the great council room, feigning interest in barley yield and wool counts.

Each time Colyne proudly introduced Ihon to people of neighboring villages and placed his hand on his back, Ihon willed his muscles not to recoil, not to move his shoulder violently to shake off the burning touch.

Ihon sat up late at night in a high-backed chair, near the fire, while Colyne spoke of legacy and strengthening ties with neighboring clans and all that they could do together. He felt a twisted satisfaction, a perverse pleasure, each time Colyne expressed joy in their togetherness. It was far too easy to deceive Colyne, who was a fool bent on the belief that brotherhood, that blood alone, created bonds of loyalty.

When the day came to renew the clan's pledge of loyalty to the Laird and Chieftain of the castle, the great hall was filled with the scent of burning pine and oiled leather, the floor covered in fresh rushes, and the stone walls echoing with the solemn murmur of tradition. The clansmen gathered proudly in full regalia. Their tartan plaids draped over their shoulders, and their blades fastened at their sides. Each man was wearing their family brooch, bearing crests, and polished to gleam in the dim torchlight.

Ihon stepped forward first; he made sure of that, feeling bold as ever. He knelt before Colyne with a precise flourish, his hand pressed to his heart, his voice steady as he swore fealty. His words rang clear beneath the vaulted ceiling, and every eye in the hall took note. The younger brother's tone held just the right quiver of reverence, just the right weight of affection. A model of loyalty, a brother's bond made sacred in the eyes of kinship.

And yet, inside, Ihon shuddered with derision. His tongue bitter with the taste of each false word, but oh, what a fool his brother was! Blind with trust, puffed with pride. And oh, what fools these men and women were, lapping up the pageantry like hounds at the foot of the table. Ihon's chest swelled with manic pride. He saw every glance, every gesture, confirming his convincing performance.

Ihon was ruthless and deliberate; his plan was flawless. His narcissism smothered any thought of failure, and his ambition beat loud beneath his ribs like a war drum. He was ready.

IV.

The moon, a mere sliver in the sky, gave no light. Ihon had planned his malevolent deed with stone-hearted care. He had waited patiently for the cycle to bring the darkest of nights. Heavy clouds gathered, their murky blackness further covering the moon, a silent omen that the moment was right.

The castle lay still, dark, and cold. The servants long ago retired, resting their heads on straw-filled pillows, behind thick wooden doors. The hearths had burned to smoldering embers, casting no warmth as the chill of the night crept steadily forward.

Ihon walks next to the wall, his fingers trailing along the frozen stone. An intoxicating delirium threatens to overtake his senses. *Tonight,* the hatred festering in his heart will at last be satisfied. *Tonight,* his bloodthirsty soul will be granted its long-awaited salve. His thirst will be quenched, finally. Tremors of excitement quake through him. He grins in silence, knowing the voices that have haunted the chasms of his mind will finally be unleashed, raining down upon those he hates most.

As he turns down the longest passageway leading to Colyne's chambers, Ihon's pulse quickens. In his hand, he carries a family heirloom, a dagger passed down through generations of the Doomfrys clan. He has spent hours grinding its edge against stone, sparks of rage flying like embers of fate. The blade is now sharp. Perfect. His mouth waters like a beast before the kill. He has imagined this moment a hundred times, the gleam of the dagger, the give of flesh, the blade entering his prey, the silence that will follow. To Ihon, this blade is more than steel; it's the potency he craves, dominance at last fulfilled. When Colyne lies cold and lifeless, *everything* will be his.

With a shiver of anticipation, Ihon drags the blade lightly along the wall. A soft scratching sound follows him down the musty corridor.

In his mind, Ihon prepares for the kill. He forces himself to pull the blade from the wall and put the dagger back into his sleeve. He's almost upon the secret door, only accessible through this hidden passage. The door that will allow him to be a dreadful ghost. He will come and go without notice or sound. The darkness is engulfing, but Ihon knows exactly where he is.

Doomfrys' Castle is riddled with hidden and forgotten mazes, like the memory of a madman, twisted, looping, and impossible to map. Ihon, long left alone to wander the webs of stone, knows them like the spider that spun them.

Behind the wall of the elder brother's chamber lies a narrow passage, once designed to ensure the chieftain's safety should the castle ever fall to enemies. It leads to an underground tunnel meant to hasten Colyne's escape in times of danger. But Ihon laughs at the irony! Instead, this passage of safety will become the path to Colyne's death, as his murderer walks it now to reach his room unseen.

Ihon pushes slowly against the weight of the hidden door. It groans faintly on its hinges, just a whisper of sound. A wave of warm air brushes his face, a stark contrast to the chill in his blood, as he creeps inside. Every stalking step, every foot placement, is gentle.

The dying fire in the hearth gives him just enough light to see his brother's body upon the bed. Colyne is deep in sleep, lying on his back. Ihon smiles as he takes one step, then two, closer and closer to the bed.

The dagger is once more in his hand, and now held up in his fist, ready to slice. As Ihon stands over his brother's vulnerable form, the hate and jealous rage he has held onto for so long seems to shoot through the tensed muscles of his arms and hands. His blood pumps fast through his veins, and the pounding of it echoes so loudly in his ears that he must focus to grip the knife steadily. This is his chance.

Ihon raises the dagger above his head. Just as he is about to plunge the blade downward, Colyne's eyes flutter open. For a split second, brother stares at brother, Ihon's eyes filled with anger and malice, Colyne's with confusion and surprise. Ihon freezes, startled by this unexpected moment of truth, but then a cruel satisfaction washes over him. To see his strong, faultless brother utterly afraid is more gratifying than he ever imagined.

Before Colyne can react, Ihon slams the blade downward, driving it into his brother's chest. It slides in easily, almost too easily, and barely makes a sound. As Colyne jerks and wheezes in pain, Ihon slashes again and again. He hears the crunch of bone and the puncture of lung.

Colyne grips Ihon's wrist, but he is too weak to stop the motion, the angle is all wrong, and his blood is quickly leaving his body. Foamy blood sputters from Colyne's lips as he labors to speak. His quiet rasp of *"Ihon, why...."* hangs in the air, before his final gasps are choked off into silence.

Colyne's fingers slip from Ihon's sleeve and fall limply to the bed with a soft thump.

Ihon lingers, staring at what he's done. A part of him itches to light a candle to see the full horror, to drink in the carnage in every detail. But the flicker of cowardice, that ever-burning instinct to protect his own skin, pushes him back. He retreats slowly, step by step, until his spine presses against the cold stone where the hidden door stands ajar.

With calculated care, he uses his blood-free, "clean" hand to slip through, pulling the panel shut behind him. With a soft click, he has escaped through the doorway.

And then... he laughs. Silent at first, then wicked and giddy, the sound swells into a bubbling hysteria, a blend of delight and madness, as he runs barefoot down the narrow, damp corridor toward the safety of his chambers.

His brother is dead! The castle, his father's lands, the admiration of the village, and the loyalty of the clan, all of it will be his.

What a glorious night.

He lifts his bloodied hand to his face and inhales. The iron scent floods his senses. A shiver of wicked ecstasy coils through his chest. Colyne is dead. And Ihon is more alive than ever before.

V.

Colyne lies silent as the grave while Ihon escapes. His instincts desperately urging him to scream at the physical pain, to move, to flinch. But he doesn't, he knows he must feign death so that he might live long enough to fight against his brother, if there is any justice left in the world. He must play dead to survive just a few moments longer.

As soon as he hears the soft bump of the secret panel sealing back into place, he tightens his grip on his thrashed and torn nightshirt, pulling it tight around his body to hold his guts in and to keep torn flesh together. It is in vain, for as he presses against the savage wounds inflicted by his brother, the gaping tears ooze blood, and his body quickly loses warmth.

He catches his breath and steels his nerves.

Ihon, why? His brother's look, the hatred in his eyes, replays in his mind. The moment the blade flashed in the dim light and plunged into his body was not as sharp as the knowing who caused it. Colyne shivers all over, and the pain is blinding, but it is the betrayal that hurts the most.

Colyne forces himself upright, agony through every fiber as he stands. Overcome with the pain, he drops to his knees. He must make it to the door, where his manservant waits on the other side. Crawling now, dragging his body and leaving a smear of blood in his wake, his hand fumbles for the door. He feebly pounds against it.

"My lord?" The trusted manservant asks, muffled through the door.

The door creaks open, and Crawford enters with a flickering candle that allows Colyne to catch the horror in the man's eye at his broken form.

With his last thread of strength, Colyne lifts his head and, through his ragged breath, declares, "Crawford, Ihon has done it. He has betrayed me, betrayed us all. He has murdered me..."

The words spill from his bloodied lips like a final confession, then weakness overtakes him, and he lies limp at his servant's feet.

VI.

Ihon lies in bed, taking deep, deliberate inhales to quiet the adrenaline coursing through his veins. His blood-soaked clothes smolder in the fire, hissing and popping as the evidence burns up. The windows, thrown open wide, pull the smoky fog from the fire out into the chilled night.

Ihon had hastily pulled a clean nightshirt over his head before lying down in his bed. He must appear at peace, undisturbed, when the servants burst in with their frantic cries.

"Someone has murdered Laird Colyne," they will shout, horror-struck, when they discover his lifeless body. They will turn to Ihon for guidance, leadership, *for justice.* Just as he planned.

He will feign shock when he is awakened by the shouts of servants. Ihon practices moving his face into sadness, and then a look of panic and terror. Yes, he will be convincing.

Ihon closes his eyes in delight, thinking he has hours before his dead brother is found.

But only moments pass before a thunder of footsteps echoes down the hallway, rushing straight towards his chambers. He stiffens, no, he prepares. The moment of his grandeur has arrived. He will be the devoted brother first, roused from slumber, filled with despair, and he will thrash around in disbelief. He will wail, collapse, and then turn to anger, demanding answers.

The door bursts open. His lips part, ready to ask, "What? What has happened?" But the words never leave his mouth because the men do not stop; they storm into the room and yank him roughly from his bed before he can even cry out.

Ihon struggles to get his footing as he is dragged from the room and is finally able to muster the words, despite the authentic surprise. "What is this? Why do you treat me so? What has happened?" he screams at them.

The servants remain silent, jaws set and unreadable. They restrain Ihon, as his bare feet rush against the stone floor to keep up. They force him forward.

Only when they pass the main hall and begin to ascend the cold, narrow steps toward the North Tower does a flicker of concern pierce Ihon's chest.

The North Tower, rising high above the rest of the castle, has always served but one grim purpose. A cage. A place of silence and rot. A death chamber reserved for betrayers to the clan.

Panic begins to claw its sharp fingers through Ihon's chest, scratching its way up his throat. Ihon resists, pushing back against the men who have known him all his life. But their arms grip him unyieldingly, merciless. Despite his thrashing, they pull him up the winding stairs leading to the tower.

When his protests are ignored, Ihon demands answers. "What is this? What is happening?"

Still, no one speaks; they yank at his body harsher.

Then the heavy door at the top groans open, and without ceremony, Ihon is shoved into the solitary circular room. He stumbles to a stop, eyes wide and frantic. *This was not part of the plan!*

There, on a litter by the far wall, lies Colyne. Ashen-faced, pain-riddled, and shivering, but he's unmistakably alive.

Ihon gasps, frozen in alarm. "No.." he breaths.

This can't be. Colyne *cannot* be alive! The blows were fatal. He saw the tear of skin; he saw the damage. His plan was flawless! Ihon rubbed his eyes and looked again, knowing that he would wake up to the ending he had planned, but Colyne's mournful stare still pierced him.

Colyne whispers, between gasps of air, each shallow breath a fight against death, "Ihon, it didn't have to be this way. This ending."

Ihon stares at him, sees the mangled body, and for a flicker of a moment, he feels it. *The thrill. The power* of standing over his broken brother. But then he looks up.

The servants. The clansmen. Their faces are carved with fury, their eyes brimming with betrayal and fuming anger. Their silence screams their damning accusations.

Suddenly, Ihon's cowardly heart takes hold. He looks to his brother with craven eyes, voice shaking, "Colyne, save me, brother. Forgive me, have mercy!"

The room offers no mercy. No saving. Only judgment.

Colyne gives his brother one final look before whispering to the witnesses. "It was him," he groans. "My brother is a murderer. He cannot lead this clan. The castle cannot be left to him."

Heavy silence smothers the room. All eyes are fixed on Colyne as his eyes flutter and then close forever. They hear the last rattling breath leaving his mutilated lungs.

No sooner had the sigh of death been released from Colyne's body did the servants grasp tighter to Ihon. Their hands became claws, tearing and shredding the fine fabric from his frame.

Ihon's screams ring out, shrill and frantic. Terrified, then angry. His fear mixes with stubborn, unrepentant screams. Words laced with hate and fury spew from his lips.

The clansmen seize Ihon's flailing arms and wrench them above his head, binding them tight. As clan law permits, they draw their blades, sharp and merciless, and begin the brutal work of justice. A traitor to the clan must be cut and disemboweled while he wiggles and writhes in pain.

Ihon twists and convulses in agony. The torture overtakes him, and scream after scream tears from his throat, but not of regret, only indignation.

He curses them. He curses Colyne. He curses the clan and the castle.

"I lay curses on you all!" he screams, though his voice falters. Through clenched teeth, but a chilling whisper, they hear Ihon's last words, "I will haunt these lands until even the stones bleed. My name will be carved into your nightmares. There will be no peace here, not now. Not ever."

The clansmen shudder at the darkness of the curse. Ihon's mangled body finally collapses. They allow grief and rage to drive the final act of this bloody punishment. They do not relish such grisly work.

They stab Ihon in turn, driving their blades into his chest, branding him a traitor with each pierce of their blade. They drag his motionless form to the turret of the north tower and hurl his body over the low stone wall.

Barely conscious as he falls, Ihon realizes, in a twist of fate, that his last sight in this earthly form is the beloved sliver moon.

With a thud and a wet, sickening puncture, Ihon lands on the thick fence, skewered through by a pole spike.

The servants turn from the gory scene, hands bloodied and their faces pale. Masculine bellows of pain rise through the castle, raw and guttural, sounds of grief for their fallen laird. The mourning cries echo down the spiral staircase of the North Tower, rousing every soul within the stone walls.

The night has claimed two men's lives. One elder, one younger; one untarnished, one evil. Yet Ihon's dying curses linger, still alive. His phantom rage clings to the air, whispers of his vengeance seem to reverberate off the walls, and into the men's minds. Even as the men carry Colyne's lifeless body far, far from the cursed North Tower, the dark whispers of Ihon's blasphemies follow them, refusing to be shaken from their souls.

VII.

The clansmen and villagers mourned deeply. Even in Scotland's rich and violent history, filled with feuds and vengeful acts amongst the highland and lowland clans, this act of fratricide shocked all who heard the tale. The impact of the murder was a great thunderclap above their heads and a ringing in their ears.

Their father received the message deep in the Highlands: both his sons, his only heirs, were now buried in the land of his inheritance. One righteous son lay to rest in the churchyard, honored and mourned. But his father's heart also lamented for his lost son, Ihon, whose final resting place was nowhere at all.

The last cruel, insulting punishment for traitors was to be cast out into the wild, where beasts might scatter their bones, unworthy of even a shallow grave. This was Ihon's fate.

Poor Mavis, the Chieftain thought bitterly. She would have wanted both her sons lying beside her in the churchyard. Side by side in death as they were in youth.

Now, being of old age and heirless, the Chieftain of Doomfrys felt his fire extinguish within himself. He no longer desired to guard his lands. He no longer wanted to lead his people into battle. He had failed his most sacred duty to protect his sons. He had never thought the charge would require him to protect them from each other.

Thus, upon taking to his bed, the Chieftain knew he would not rise again. A great fever ate away at the little strength left, and the clansmen understood that soon they would count three deaths due to Ihon's degeneracy.

The castle grew heavy with shadow. It cast ghouls on every wall. And when the father finally succumbed to death, disembodied and mournful cries haunted the night, sending shivers down both clansmen's and women's spines, and striking fear in their hearts.

Were these muffled cries from Colyne's soul, still weeping at the betrayal of his younger brother? Or was it their father, groaning in the depths of grief? Or perhaps it was Mavis, crying out in wrath across the unseen plains.

Yet, on other nights, it was not sorrow they heard, but the voice of Ihon riding the wind in curses, echoing with vengeance, venom creeping from the stairs of the North tower. Razor-edged threats seeped from the passageways hidden between the walls, relentless whispers laced with malice. The castle had never known such cold.

In the darkness of night, the castle groaned and shuddered. The servants locked their doors, pulled their covers over their heads, and burrowed deep. In the day, they quietly crept through the gloom-filled halls, now as lifeless as the master they had lost.

In time, even the most loyal clansmen could no longer endure life at Doomfrys. Their devotion to the Chieftain ran deep, but their minds frayed. Sanity slipped away from them with each sleepless night and each haunting day.

The castle had become unbearable. So, with heavy hearts, they sealed it. All the thick wooden doors were locked, and their iron latches bolted tight.

They joined their kin in the highlands. Abandoning the Scottish border to its fate, whatever God willed that to be. With every step, they whispered prayers, not only for safety, but for vengeance. Should any enemy dare breach the gates, let them be consumed by the frenzied madness festering within those walls. Let the ghosts rise; let the castle drive them to ruin.

Thus, Doomfrys Castle sat, its hallways full of heirlooms and faded plaids, but utterly void of life for decades upon decades. Of course, it was looted, thieves took what they could, and time did its work with rock eaten away by winds and rain.

Yet, the castle's formidable presence endured. An unseen force cast a protective veil over it, holding the walls upright, the rooms eerily empty, and the silence unnervingly alive.

The story of Colyne and Ihon, two proud Scottish brothers, handsome and strong, echoed through generations. Over time, the story swelled beyond memory, climbing to the heights of pure fantasy until the true tale withered into fable, then faded into myth.

Eventually, the Doomfrys clan claimed use of the old castle once more. But no one, no heir to the bloodline, lingered long inside its walls. The years marched on, but Doomfrys remained emptier than full, haunted more by silence than life, at least from those with warm blood flowing in their veins.

Finally, in 1649, more than two hundred years after the death of Chieftain Colyne and his sons, the last living heir of Doomfrys resolved to cast off the ghosts of the past. The Highlands and the lowlands were theirs no more. England now reigned over the clans, and the old ways crumbled. There was nothing left.

James Doomfrys and his wife, Elizabeth, chose exile in the New World. They sealed the great doors of the castle and turned their backs for good, vowing never to return to the constant dread and shadow of Doomfrys Castle that had filled their hearts and darkened their souls.

As each league of the sea carried them farther from Doomfrys, a strange lightness returned to them, a loosening of something vile and diseased that had clung to their blood for generations. They landed in Virginia, in the New World, and with the strength and resolve of their Scottish heritage, they forged a new life, one of peace, purpose, and quiet prosperity.

PART TWO

VIII.

England – 1945

My hope rises with the sun today. The war is finally over. Germany has admitted defeat and surrendered. Hitler is dead. We are back in Nottingham, England. And for the first time in what seems like forever, I have a sense that my life can begin again.

Normally, we'd be up by now, sweating through a rigorous run and PT training, but our commanding officer must be feeling generous considering the recent "victory." No bugle has blasted reveille to announce rise and shine and tear us from our sleep. Still, my eyes snap open at the first hint of light, whether it's a flashlight, high explosives, or the morning sun. They say soldiers learn to sleep through anything, but not me.

I glance around at the row of soldiers in the massive barracks hall. It's only half full now. I try not to think about how crowded it was when we arrived here, years ago, when every cot was taken, and every man was filled with fire and righteous indignation. All the empty spaces in the barracks remind me that we were ready to fight, but not ready to die.

We were a group of overzealous paratroopers back then, eager, proud, and naive. All thrilled, me included, to be in the 82nd Airborne Division, the first of America's airborne.

We trained at Camp Clairborne, Louisiana, before moving to Fort Bragg, where I was assigned to the 504th PIR, or Parachute Infantry Regiment. From there, Europe became our battleground, starting in Italy. After a few long years, in February of 1944, I was asked to transfer to the 507th. That's when I first sat in this very barracks hall.

Preparation for Operation Neptune was brief but intense. We dropped into Normandy, and for thirty-three days, we fought without pause in France. It wasn't until July that we were finally pulled back to England.

I look around at the sparser 507th now. Most of them are still asleep, sleeping the kind of sleep only those who have lived without it can. Members of my jump team are scattered in their cots around me. Jones is snoring lightly in the cot next to mine.

While Jones is newer to the 507th, he was no greenhorn. He'd seen his fair share of battles. We've been through a lot. We are battle brothers, he and I. A bond you can't put into words. We are thankful to be together, but also anxious to separate. I itch to have my own space again. My own air to breathe. A natural loner, I guess.

Said simply, I'm tired. Tired of noise. Tired of standing in endless lines for chow (when there was any to be had). And painfully weary of military green.

I grew up in the forests of Virginia. I was often alone in the woods, just me and the trees. That's the green I want to see again. As a child, I listened to the birds cawing overhead and stared at the sky through the sun-soaked branches. I'd lie for hours, listening to the river speak its flowing language. That, that peace, is what I consider my real home.

But for the last three years, my life has been the roar of planes, the crack of bullets cutting through the air, and the final sound of a man's sigh of death before dying next to me, eyes wide open.

I'm lucky. I know that. After Normandy, we were dropped into the Ardennes Forest in December. The winter of 1944 was brutal and deadly. Many from our team didn't make it. Others did, but carry scars worse than death, even extreme psychological trauma. There was physical damage as well from exposure. Some lost fingers, toes, and even ears to the freezing conditions.

Later, they'd call it one of the "roughest and deadliest" winters that region had ever seen. I believe they got that right.

At night, when the cold bit down into my frozen bones, I'd close my eyes and drift back to Virginia, back to the thick, humid warmth of home. I'd see lightning bugs flickering in my dreams, wings fluttering behind my eyelids, and I took it as a good omen. I'd will myself to stay warm, hold onto that image, and just stay alive till morning.

Finally, in May of 1945, we met up with the Russian forces as Germany surrendered. From there, we became the occupation force in Berlin. The papers back home, in America, started calling us "America's Guard of Honor," but most of us didn't feel honorable. We just wanted to go home.

However, I am resolute; I will not leave Europe with only war-torn, blood-soaked memories to carry home. I need something between my life at home and death. A buffer. Like a sponge to soak up the ache and wring it out, separating it from *my Virginia.*

I've decided: when my walking papers are given, I'll stay in England for a while. I'll see the English countryside, maybe even the highlands of Scotland, to be reminded that joyful life still exists beyond ruin. I fought hard for mankind; now it's time to fight just as hard for my own humanity.

Nature heals me, it always has. I hope with time, it will heal me again, and when my feet step on American soil, I'll carry the memory of England's green hills, and not the trenches of France or the smoke-filled sky stinging my eyes as I fell from it.

When people ask what it was like *"over there,"* I'll tell them this: there was beauty. That's what I'll say, nothing more. There is no glory in taking lives, and I've come to understand that those who've seen the most are the ones least likely to speak about it.

England draws me in. The first time I set foot here, it felt odd in some way, like I was getting closer to something important. At first, it was the fight or the fray of battle. But now, even with battles behind me and the end of the war, that feeling of longing remains in my gut.

So, I'll stay on. I have sufficient money saved. All that combat pay went straight to the bank. What's there to spend it on when your days are spent jumping out of planes or crouching in trenches? It's enough to last me a year or so, if I'm careful. I don't need much. I'm used to sleeping under the stars, and anything tastes better than army rations.

I'll travel light, just my sleeping bag, a few civilian clothes, my army-issued supply kit, a flashlight, some medical supplies, and the Colt M1911 .45 issued to me back at boot camp.

I'm lost in my thoughts when Jones's muted voice cuts through the quiet. He turns over, wide awake, and says a little louder, "Cornell."

"Jones," I reply.

It's our routine morning greeting. In the foxholes, it was less about civility and more about survival. Just a confirmation that we were both still breathing.

Jones stretches and sits up on his cot.

"Today's the day, Cornell," he says.

I nod.

He lets out a slow breath and continues, "We won't belong to the U.S. government anymore."

I nod again.

My lack of articulation, my silence, grates on Jones, but he's used to it. I'm a listener rather than a talker. That's part of why they chose me as the unit's sniper, for my ability to be still and to listen. I can observe and be patient.

As a sniper, my movements are slow and steady, but when the moment comes, my natural fight instinct is fast and precise. Over time, the rhythm of my heartbeat became my pacer. Looking through the scope of my sniper rifle, I carefully count each beat, keeping my breathing calm, my hands steady, and my aim precise. Then I wait.

"I can go home and marry Beth," Jones says with a grin. "And you can go... well, whatever it is you're going to do."

He's making light of my plans, but in a good-natured way. He knows there's no family anymore or a girl to return home to. Jones said simply, *"A good walk never hurt nobody, I guess,"* when I told him I'd be staying on in England.

We rose and began folding our sleeping equipment.

Dog stood up and looked at me expectantly. He's a parachute-trained, army-issued canine, and we've been through a lot together. I did practice jumps with him when he was just a pup, tucked safely in my cargo pockets back in Louisiana. Somehow, I managed to keep him with me all this time.

Not knowing what to name him, I've always called him Dog. I told myself it was better that way, not getting too attached. Service canines don't often make it out of battle. Despite my attempts to stay neutral, Dog was mine. We both knew it.

His warm body would curl up beside me in the freezing foxholes of the Ardennes, surrounded by the dark woods. Dog's warmth is probably why I kept all my toes. His attentiveness, his upright ears, and the way his nose would point straight forward whenever danger crept near all became my early warning system. He would signal to me silently, and I would act accordingly. In more ways than one, Dog kept me sane.

But then Dog and I were nearly blown up by a landmine. He was injured too, but still whined and tugged at my arm until I regained consciousness. I walked away with a broken arm, but something deeper in Dog broke; he lost his nerve. Dog lost his courage.

Maybe that's why the Army commission board approved my request to take Dog home with me. When I reported that he visibly shook on perimeter checks, they said he was done. Retired. Taking Dog off their hands was doing them a favor, I figured. And I owe Dog that.

To the men in our unit, Dog was more than a mascot. He was a brave, loyal warrior. But by the end, we all identified with his broken spirit.

"Sit, Dog," I say.

The German Shepherd obediently sits. His eyes stay locked on me, aware of my every move.

I pack up my gear. Might as well be prepared for release tomorrow. In the same orderly fashion, we were taught back in boot camp, I line everything up neatly beside the cot, ready to go.

"Let's go, Dog."

I step out of the barracks, heading toward the mess hall. Dog falls into place, one step to my side and one step behind. I hear the soft, familiar panting as we walk into the sunlight. Speaking isn't necessary; he'd follow me anywhere.

IX.

"Sergeant Cornell!" boomed the voice of my commanding officer, Lieutenant Parley. He wanted to meet with each of us to "have a check-in." I'd spent most of the morning in the hallway of the cramped office building. As they say in the military, *Hurry up and wait.*

"Sir!" I respond, standing at attention.

"Sergeant Michael Cornell," he repeats, motioning me to sit.

I take the chair opposite him and try not to squirm. Finally, he sits down himself, elbows on the desk, hands pressed together, and fingers steepled in front of him.

"You'll be leaving as an E5, battlefield promotions no less," he says, glancing at the papers in front of him. "Paratrooper, and experience as an army sniper. Uncle Sam's invested a lot in you."

He looks up. "You've had quite the career during the war here."

I nod. Calling it a "career" doesn't sit right with me. One year of training and three years in Europe doing what I had to do? No. I couldn't bring myself to say as much, so I remain silent. I did my duty.

The Lieutenant wasn't finished yet. He stood and began pacing behind his chair. I suspect he's about to deliver a speech he'd already given a dozen times today.

"You've trained hard and progressed through the ranks with admirable speed," he began. "I'd like to make you an offer. Stay on, Sergeant. Make the military your career. I see a commissioned officer in your future."

Lieutenant Parley pauses, gesturing with a sweep of his left hand across the desk. "We need men like you to keep our military strong, to make sure *this* never happens again."

By *"this,"* he means the war. Hitler. All the death. I watch the motion of his hand and feel a twinge of guilt at my skepticism. Of course, *this* would happen again—humans and their short memories.

"Thank you, sir, for the words of encouragement," I say. "However, a career in the military isn't for me. I've made other plans."

He seems taken aback. "What plans?" he asks. "I heard about your brother, Sergeant. Africa, was it? Parents too. That's a blow. A terrible blow. To be away at war and lose a brother in battle and lose your parents to sickness..." He shakes his head. "But now you've got a family here, your brothers."

"Thank you, sir. But I have to say no." I pause and clear my throat. "Sir, I'd like to be discharged here. I want to stay in England for a while. No orders back to the States."

I keep it vague. Giving only the barest information. No need to explain to a career military man that I'm off to find my sanity again.

"Sergeant Cornell, I can arrange that for you. As a special favor, mind you, don't go spreading the word around. But I'll only do it on one condition: that you give my offer some thought. Let's say six months leave, with plans to rejoin us at Fort Bragg after you've had some time. Whole new military contract, see. Will you think about it?"

"Sir, I will not re-enlist."

I say it plainly, meeting his gaze head-on. He stares back, squinting slightly, as if weighing whether I am resolute or open to persuasion. His face twitches, and mine remains still as stone.

"Okay, Sergeant, I see you're determined. It's a crying shame, though, you know, a damn shame. You've got talent. Raw talent, and we can't train that. I watched the men look to you, even before some of their superiors. You've got grit, and the good sense to act quickly."

"Thank you, sir."

"Stop thanking me. It's just the truth."

He stands, and I follow his lead. He reaches across the desk to deliver a firm handshake. "I'll have your discharge papers ready by zero nine hundred, tomorrow. Stop by my office on your way out."

"Thank you, sir. Thank you for everything." Not knowing what else to say, I salute and step out.

Relief hits me like a warm wave. I am out of the army as of 0900 tomorrow. Finally, my journey can begin, head towards whatever's calling me north.

I hope it's peace, that it's a full night's rest with both eyes closed. I can't explain it, but something is coming.

Dog stands at attention outside, near the office door. His face pointed directly at the entrance, waiting for me. He is a better soldier than I will ever be.

"Dog, come."

I don't look back. I know he's following.

X.

It's been a month of wandering. After walking to the train station from the base in Nottingham, I decided to see London before heading north. Dog and I boarded the first southbound train, crammed into a tight compartment with civilians and a few soldiers like me, discharged and floating in the mid-space between now and what might come next.

The people in London were kind and helpful, despite having been through so much. Some even slipped scraps of bread crust or little bits of meat to Dog. They would pat his head and say things like, *"That's a good boy,"* as if he had done something to earn the treats besides standing steady, with big brown eyes and a hopeful wagging tail.

The old city was broken and blackened by bombs. Sadly, it gave me little reason to stay. The skyline sagged, and entire blocks had been reduced to hollow brick shells and charred beams.

In London, I saw children who smiled happily as they played handball in the street, nimbly dodging piles of brick and glass as they chased after runaway throws. Their resiliency inspired me. I'll admit that in some ways the sight nearly moved me to tears.

Rebuilding was happening, apparent through the echoing hammers banging against nails, and the trucks carrying away rubble. The city overflowed with hope for a new day, and yet for me it smelled faintly of TNT and gunpowder. Probably just my imagination, but it wasn't for me. I decided to head to the open country.

Dog and I took the northbound train from London, no real destination, just to wherever it was going next. I'd told myself we'd get off whenever the prompting nudged me. That led to brief stops in Cambridge and Leicester, enough time to stretch our legs and buy a sandwich.

We spent most of our time outside the big cities, where the fields stretched out before us, all green and expansive.

Now, I sit on a train from Leicester to York. I aimlessly gaze out the window while Dog sleeps curled at my feet. My pack rests beside me. It's ragged and worn but still able to transport all my meager belongings.

The train car is half full of villagers, businessmen sprinkled in singles and pairs. A mother in a neatly pressed pink dress boards with two children in tow. She enters the car and gives me a polite nod, a half-smile, and gently tells her children to "Step lively," as they shuffle into the row just ahead of me.

My gaze turns from the window to the children, then back to the window again. The countryside scrolls past. Little thatches of towns scattered across fields and rolling hills, interrupted occasionally by a stone wall or railway landing.

The little girl turns around in her seat and locks eyes with me. I stare back. She doesn't blink. Her clear, blue eyes keep studying me.

I don't know what to say to children, and barely know what to say to adults. So, I stare back.

"Are you a soldier? Is that your dog?" the girl asks, her voice echoing off the train walls, loud and bright.

"Daphne, sit down," her mother demands just as loudly. Dog stirs at my feet, lifts his head, ears twitching. I pat him reassuringly.

"No problem, ma'am," I mumble.

But the little girl doesn't sit down. She keeps her eyes on me and lifts a well-loved teddy bear, grasped between her little, petite fingers.

"This is Fuzzy," she announces.

"Hello, Fuzzy," I say.

"Daphne..." Her mother sighs, the long, tired sigh of every mother resigned to the constancy of children.

The little girl swings her bear in front of my face, close enough that I catch the faint scent of soap on her hands, something floral, clinging to her skin.

The train rattles sharply as we cross a rough patch of track and slip into a tunnel. The lights flicker.

Fuzzy slips from Daphne's hand and drops directly onto Dog's head. Dog lifts his eyes without raising his head, then lowers them again, as if he's as resigned as the girl's mother.

"Oh, Daphne, you are bothering this nice gentleman," her mother chides, her voice now low and apologetic rather than irritated.

It's then that the little boy, who has been quietly absorbed in a picture book, stands and says with responsible seriousness, "I'll get it for Daphne, Mother."

He steps around the seat and into my aisle. He moves with careful politeness; obviously, he's been taught to mind his manners. He bends to retrieve the bear, but I've already rescued Dog by scooping the bear off his head.

"Thank you, sir, my sister loves this toy," he says, lifting his face to mine.

Instantly, I see Sean. The same blue eyes. Wide, honest, and unburdened. My fingers loosen without meaning to, and the bear drops again.

The boy looks at me questioningly as I pick up Fuzzy yet again and hand it to him for a second time.

"Sorry, sir, to bother you," the boy says softly.

"No," I say, trying to steady my voice. "No bother. You're a good brother."

XI.

Outskirts of Wytheville, Virginia – 1930

"Sean, you're walking too fast," I say, pumping my legs to keep up.

"Oh, Mikey," he calls back, grinning. "There are always two ways of looking at it. Maybe you're not walking fast *enough*."

It's summer, and we have no school to dictate our schedule, yet Sean still can't help speeding ahead. He moves his long legs, well, longer than mine at least, like he's racing someone.

He teases me sometimes when I start taking giant steps to match his stride; he calls me a camel or a stiff-legged toy soldier. It doesn't bother me. I'd never admit it, but I want to be like him in every way.

He slows down and ruffles my hair, something anyone else would get a black eye for. Instead of punching, I twist my head away and swat at his hand, but not too hard.

"Where are we goin' anyway?" I whine.

"To our rock."

The sun isn't even up yet, and we're already five miles from home. Sean always wants to watch it rise from our special place. It's just ours. He calls it the *Appalachian Vacation.* I call it a long walk.

We are still in the dog days of the season, and the mountains call to us like an old friend. The thick scent of oak and pine fills our nostrils, earthly and pure, bolstering our young souls with every breath.

Sean carries a handkerchief with two sandwiches wrapped snug inside, swinging it casually back and forth. He never lets me eat mine until after sunrise. Mama made them early this morning. She uses thick slices of her homemade bread, crusty on the outside, but so soft in the middle. That bread fills out most of our meals, heavy and filling, with whatever meat or jam we have available piled high in the middle. Today I saw her spooning fresh strawberry jam, made from the berries in our garden. It's my favorite.

"Again?" I whine.

"Yes, Mikey, again," Sean says, making a goofy face at me. "Why go anywhere else this time of day? You know the sunrise looks best from our rock."

"Fine." This is our routine: me trying to seem uninterested, and Sean knowing that I would follow him anywhere.

We wind our way through thick, clinging grass, shrubs, and wildflowers to the top of the hill, where our favorite trees and our rock nestle against the slope, overlooking the Blue Ridge Mountains stretching north and south.

We always face east on our rock, where stripes of gold, yellow, and hints of red along the horizon have started to transform the sky.

Papa used to sit on this rock with us. He was the first to show us the way here. He also taught us how to spit sunflower seed shells off the short cliff on the far side of the rock. We didn't tell Mama about that.

But Papa starts his day much earlier now, working at the Law Office, where he tries to help people find jobs. He doesn't come with us anymore. Mama says that he ought to give up his practice, since he does very little legal work anyway, and "just become a saint already."

I'm not exactly sure what she means, but it doesn't sound like a compliment the way she says it.

Sometimes, if we sit still enough, we'll see a red fox or a coyote dart past, sniffing the ground in search of their early morning meal. Once, we even spotted a black bear and her cub moving along the next ridge over. Their dark forms moved quietly and gracefully in the morning light. That surprised me. We didn't tell Mama about that either.

Day strikes the mountain peaks first, sharp with bright light, slowly oozing down onto the hills and valleys like warm honey. We sit quietly and just watch. I wonder what Sean is thinking about, but I don't ask. He told me once it's a crime to interrupt a thinking man in nature.

So, instead, I practice being a thinking man.

Really, I just look around a lot and think about chasing squirrels on the way home, or maybe stopping by the creek for a dip, or trying to catch a brook trout with my hands. Sean's caught one three times! I'm still practicing.   Finally,   when the sunlight starts to burn up our bare knees, Sean speaks. "Okay, Mikey. Let's go."

I hop off the rock while he shakes out the red handkerchief, crumbs flying into the breeze, then carefully folds it into his pocket.

We work our way back down the shrubby hillside.

"It's Mama's birthday today," Sean says. "Let's see if we can find any leftover spring flowers to bring home with us. She likes those."

I groan, already knowing what that means: no time for fishing today. Instead, we'll take the long way back, through the meadow that turns into a rainbow every spring, filled with wildflowers.

The meadow isn't much of a rainbow anymore, but there are still clumps of pink, bashful wake-robins, and clusters of white woodland stonecrop dotting the field.

"They're not mama's favorites," Sean says, crouching low. "But she'll still thank us. Might even give us some cake early!"

That gets me. I'm sold. I drop to my knees and start picking. I focus on the white flowers; they grow in bigger clumps, and I figure we'll get home faster.

Then I spot a bushy patch of slightly different white flowers. They're bunched together like a ready-made bouquet. I figure I'll just yank out the root and be done with it.

But as I reach down, Sean grabs my wrist.

"No, Mikey! Danger!"

Startled, I twist my hand away and scowl at him.

"Hey!" I say, glaring at him accusingly.

"That's hemlock, buddy," he says, serious now. "One of the most poisonous plants out here. That stuff can kill you. I want you to stay away from it."

I jerk my hands away from him and back up a little.

"I wasn't going to eat it," I say, the only defense I can think of.

Sean looks at me like my third-grade teacher when she asks me a question to see if I'm paying attention, testing me.

"We've got enough now; we can go home. But first show me you know the difference," Sean says. "We'll look for hemlock on the way back home."

I groan again.

XII.

England - 1945

The train whistle pulls me out of my reverie, and I notice that both children in front of me have fallen asleep. The mother reads a magazine in peace. I step off the train. I think we'll walk from here on out.

We spend an hour winding through the streets of the city, then follow a road leading north, away from the noise and bustle of York.

The stillness of the countryside and the blue sky overhead seem to be healing, or rather, stitching up, parts of me I didn't realize were cut wide open. Besides, I can see more of the country this way, up close, along village footpaths, than I ever could through a dingy-glassed train window.

Tonight, I want stars and solitude.

A soft, grassy knoll in an open field lies out before me, a perfect place to camp for the night. Farmhouses dot the countryside, but the nearest one is at least a mile or two off. It's nearly silent with only the rustle of the tall grass and the distant sound of crickets chirping in my ears.

I lie down in the knee-deep grass, and Dog settles beside me. We can see countless stars in the sky. It's not too cold yet, so I stay on top of my sleeping bag, the air brushing my skin, cool but gentle.

With my hand resting on Dog's back, I feel the steady rise and fall of his breathing. The rhythm is familiar and calming. My eyes feel heavy, and I drift to sleep.

I walk toward a great old castle rising like a ghost from the middle of a vast, empty prairie. No buildings, no roads, only wind-whipped grass in every direction. The sky above is flat and colorless.

Two figures stand at the castle door, facing each other. They're too far to see clearly, but they are equal in height; one broad-shouldered and solid, the other is long-limbed and lean.

The thicker man folds his arms, then slowly lifts his left hand. At first, I think it's a wave. I raise my hand, about to call out. Do I know them? Have I been here before?

But he isn't waving. He's warning me. Stop.

Suddenly, I'm within arm's reach and can see them both clearly. The slender man steps forward and reaches for me. I flinch. His hand veers away, and instead, clamps around the broader man's neck.

His long fingers tighten and strangle. The choking man's eyes bulge.

I fixate on the dying man's face, then feel the aggressor's eyes burning my skin. Hate and malice, and all things evil, seep into my mind and heart. My hands go clammy; panic rises in my chest.

My mind screams: Help him! But I'm frozen. I turn away from the hateful face and catch the choking man's eyes again, red blood vessels breaking through, his arms flailing. I must do something!

And then, suddenly, it's Sean! Sean's eyes are wide with terror, his face purple and strangled. Pure panic washes through me.

I can't move! I can't help. He will die, and I can do nothing.

My body jerks awake, and I gasp. It takes a moment to catch my breath, as if I had been choked. The fear is still with me, all encompassing, thick, and suffocating. I sit up fast, heart pounding and muscles tense.

"Dog," I say, reflexively.

He's already awake, alert, and on his feet. Ears twitching, muzzle pointing at me as if the trouble is coming from my chest.

I push myself up. I need to move, to shake off the dream that still coils tight in my chest. So real, so vivid. The dream lingers in my mind, like it's still happening somewhere. Breathe. Breathe. Count to ten, I tell myself. I focus on the air filling my lungs, holding it, then slowly letting it go. I force the horrible images of Sean, bulging eyes, and the helplessness out of my mind. I clench and release my fists.

Dog stays close at my heels, silent and watchful, as I pace in a tight, irrational circle, flattening a path into the long grass.

My heart rate slows, and my reality returns, but I won't sleep anymore tonight.

I pull up my sleeping bag with shaking hands and begin rolling it. Methodically, I pack my gear, each motion routine, and grounding. Dog's ears tilt, as if questioning our early start, but I don't speak.

I keep moving, keep packing. When everything is strapped and stowed, we begin our long walk for the day.

XIII.

Around noon, we reach the city of Carlisle. We're just twenty or thirty miles from the Scottish border. Every time I pause to consider which direction to turn next, my mind whispers the same word: *north*.

I'm looking forward to Scotland; I'm eager to pick up the pace. But the nearly sleepless night and skipped breakfast are catching up to me fast.

I find a small cafe tucked along a cheerful lane and decide to stop. They serve a "full English breakfast" including eggs, sausage, tomatoes, beans, black pudding, and thick slices of bread. It's warm and is just what I didn't know I needed.

"Tea, my dear?" the waitress asks, as she sets down my white plate brimming with steaming food. Before I can answer, she tsks softly and adds with a knowing smile, "No, you're American. I'll get you some coffee in a jiff."

Surprised that he was given clearance to be at my side in the cafe, Dog is more than happy to share my food. I pat his head as he gobbles up the last of the sausage, tail thumping against the cafe floor.

Across the street stands a small, weathered building with a hand-painted sign that reads: *Historical Society Library.*

Why not? Seems like a great place to take a breather and to learn something about where we've wandered. I set my pack on the ground near the doorway, and Dog settles beside it, sitting at attention.

I step inside, and the faint scent of mold and old paper greets me, musty and familiar. I glance around the room. Bookshelves line three walls, packed with volumes from floor to low ceiling. The fourth wall breaks the organized pattern; instead of books, it's crowded with mismatched frames, each holding a photograph of faces and places from another time.

A few feet away, a dark-haired, middle-aged woman watches me with mild curiosity, as if deciding whether I'm here on purpose or by mistake. Her purple dress is faded, but clean and crisply ironed, and a well-worn apron is tied snugly around her generous waist. A feather duster rests in her hand, paused mid-task as she studies me.

"Ah, welcome! It's a slow day, you'll have the library to yourself!" she chirps.

I smile politely, though I wonder if that's true no matter when I arrive. Still, she clearly takes pride in the place. The books are neat, dust-free, and arranged by subject as best I can tell.

"Where are you coming from, young man?" she asks.

"The war," I answer reflexively.

Her smile falters. Too late, I realize she meant *where*, geographically, not *what*.

"Sorry, ma'am. I'm American. Uh, Virginia. Mind if I look around?"

Her warm smile returns at once. She beams and waves me in enthusiastically.

"Of course! Come have a look at our bit of history."

Something about her reminds me of Mama. Or maybe Aunt Geraldine. That same eagerness to tell you everything about the family and make you look at photos of relatives you never knew you had.

Even still, my interest is piqued.

"Thank you, ma'am," I say and step further inside.

The photographs vary in size and age, scattered like breadcrumbs across decades. Some are quite ancient black-and-white prints, their edges curled and yellowed with time. Others are more recent, snapshots of townsfolk during the war effort: women in aprons rolling bandages, men in uniform loading supplies. Still others capture the English countryside, a family posed before a dilapidated cottage. Children lined up outside a brick schoolhouse, a solemn priest standing before a stone church. Each picture is ordinary in its way, a quiet tribute to a village built on simplicity and hard work.

However, one photograph stands out.

It's larger, its colors nearly drained to sepia and shadow. I step closer. Beneath the image, scrawled in uneven ink, are the words: *Doomfrys Castle, Doomfrys, Scotland, 1898.*

I blink.

The photo seems to rise from the thick paper, the lines of the building sharpening as if coming alive before my eyes.

It's the castle from my dream, no, from my nightmare. The shape is unmistakable: two tall towers on either side, joined by a heavy, stony wall. It stands alone in a field, just as I remembered it. Solitary. Desolate.

I lean in, searching instinctively for the two men. My breath catches. No human figures. No trace of life. Still, a chill flickers up my spine.

Have I been there? How is this possible? I shake my head hard, trying to brush the thought away. "Nonsense," I mutter. But even as the word leaves my lips, I'm not sure I believe it.

"Excuse me?" the matron asks, a hint of offense in her voice.

"Oh, sorry, ma'am." I glance at her, trying not to sound rattled. "What do you know about this castle?"

She steps closer, peering at the photograph with the same distant curiosity. "Oh, Doomfrys? Not a great deal, I'm afraid. It's just across the border in Scotland. The Clan Doomfrys was active in that area for centuries."

She scratches her nose and adjusts her duster.

"The castle and the nearby village were significant in guarding the border, especially back when that sort of thing mattered. It's near the river Nith, if memory serves."

She frowns slightly. "Hmm, well, there's some dark story about the family, something odd, but I'm not familiar. You might find more in the parish registry, if you have time to search."

Distracted, I nod, my eyes drawn back to the unsettling photo. I want to be sure, absolutely sure that I'm not losing my mind, that it is the same.

But there it is again. The shape, the towers, the isolation. The image drags me back into the dream like quicksand. I can almost feel the air on that strange plain, hear the wind whistling around the towers.

It's the same castle. No doubt about it.

"You're interested in architecture? Then you must see these," she says, nudging me toward the far end of the wall, where pictures of old churches and statues hang in dutiful rows.

I pretend interest, murmur polite admiration, and take a few moments to stare without really seeing.

"Thank you," I say, beginning to back away.

"My pleasure," she replies, lifting her duster in a friendly wave. "Thank you for visiting our little village!"

On my way out, I glance once more at the photograph of Doomfrys Castle. A final look. But it pulls at me again. Something heavy is there, unsettling. There isn't a name for what I feel.

Dog falls into step beside me as we leave the village. I walk faster than usual, unable to shake my unease.

A few miles out, a weatherworn signpost waits at a fork in the road. Both paths lead to the Scottish border, but two choices stand before me. One points west, towards Doomfrys. The other north, to Langholm.

I don't pause, for better or worse. I turn west. Dog follows.

XIV.

Virginia - 1939

Lady Liberty's torch blazes across the movie house screen as Sean and I shuffle sideways past already-seated patrons, mumbling apologies, until we slide into the only empty seats, smack in the middle of the row.

I sigh. The newsreels are always my least favorite part of the movies, though Sean loves them.

The narrator's voice rolls out: *Ellis Island stands nearby, ready to welcome all those first greeted by the Statue of Liberty.*

The reel sweeps through a brisk tour of New York City, historic Dutch neighborhoods, Wall Street, and the mighty American Steel. I try not to yawn. After all, this is good news, as the announcer proudly declares, *"the upward movement of the nation's riches."* Not a small thing after the years of depression we'd all endured.

Still... how long until the feature starts?

I'm here for *Stagecoach*, starring John Wayne. I admire his swagger, his calm under fire, his unshakable bravery. He never seems afraid of anything.

Kind of like Sean, come to think of it.

The tour of New York fades, and a new story begins, the German and Russian invasion of Poland.

The Universal Newsreel announcer's voice sharpens: *"Adolf Hitler amasses troops."* On the screen, soldiers in perfect formation goose-step past the camera, their movements mechanical, ominous.

President Roosevelt's voice, steady and commanding, echoes through the theater. He proclaims a stance of neutrality. However, it's abundantly clear where the President's sympathy lies. The laws will be relaxed, he says, to allow the sale of arms to Great Britain.

The focus shifts back to Germany's attack on Poland. Death tolls are listed off like a laundry list, rather than real people. Dead men. Dead women. Dead children. Soldiers and civilians alike. The reel keeps playing, but the theater is silent. Not a whisper. Even Sean sits like a statue.

"It's looking really bad, Mikey," Sean whispers close to my ear, but his voice isn't low enough; people around us glance sideways, brows raised in disapproval, silently telling us to hush.

"What is, Sean?" I ask. I already know, but I want to hear Sean's point of view.

"Just going into a country like that. Killing so many. Taking what's not yours."

"Yep," I answer. It's all I can come up with. I don't know anything about Poland, or Germany, for that matter. I rely on Sean for the strong opinions and to make sense of them for me.

I've overheard quiet conversations between my parents, always low and earnest. They tend to stop if I enter the room.

Sean is relentless and certainly doesn't whisper when he talks about war. He debates fiercely. Pa mostly agrees, just to keep the peace. *Pacify Sean, so we can get through supper.*

"Strong talk like that doesn't aid digestion," Pa always says, folding his napkin into a perfect square.

Mama follows, her voice shaking, "You're right, Sean. The world has enough bullies. They're tyrants."

I don't think Mama wants to imagine another war, especially not with two sons nearing fighting age.

Seeing her distress, Pa adds softly, "We've got to protect each other."

Finally, that's when Sean will sit and let us eat.

The music swells as the movie begins, but so does Sean's voice. "I'm gonna join up, Mikey."

My eyes snap from the screen to his face. "No, Sean. President Roosevelt himself just said we're neutral! There is nothing to join!"

My voice carries louder than I mean it to, and again, heads turn with annoyed glances from the rows in front of us.

"Just watch the show," Sean says, leaning back, calm as ever. "We can talk on the way home."

But now *Stagecoach* is ruined for me.

The whole movie drags on, stretching longer with each scene. I can't focus. All I can think about is Sean leaving. Sean fighting.

For the first time, I realize how much of who I am, my identity, is wrapped up in being Sean Cornell's kid brother. He takes me everywhere. We both got jobs at the hardware store. I mostly clean up, but Sean helps customers and fills orders.

John Wayne finally delivers his last line, and the screen fades to those big white letters: *The End,* drawn across the image in all their dramatic finality. Harmonic western music swells in farewell.

We shuffle out into the bright afternoon sunlight, both raising our hands to shield our eyes. Without a word, we turn towards home. It's a couple of miles walk.

"Sean, you *can't* join," I blurt out. "Pa wants you to finish law school, and Mama will *never* let you!"

"There's time for all of that," Sean says calmly. "People are dying now. If we don't help, who will?"

"No, Sean! That's got nothing to do with us!" I plead.

He stops walking and looks at me.

"It has everything to do with us, Mikey. Remember in school, that poor kid Big Davey used to pound on last year?

How could I forget? That kid was as thin as a razor and as short as a fourth grader, although he was a freshman.

"You mean Pete Longstich?" I ask.

I remember his patched-up clothes, hanging off him like rags on a drying line. His Appalachian accent was so thick that most kids laughed when he spoke. The family didn't have a cent to their name. Everyone laughed at him. But not Sean.

"Yeah, Pete. That's his name," Sean nods. "Remember how you came home from school, eyes all red, crying because no one stepped in, not even you, when Big Davey gave him that black eye?"

I hang my head. I didn't cry, but I didn't do anything either.

"Yeah," I mutter.

"Well," Sean gives me a long look. "I bet you never want to feel like that again, right, Mikey?"

I look down, shame prickling my skin. I watch the dust plume around my shoes with each step.

The question I've been holding back for months finally tumbles out. "Was it you, Sean?"

He smiles. "Don't know what you're talking about."

But I do. Someone had put tacks under both tires of Big Davey's bicycle and painted *BULLLIES ARE COWARDS* in thick white letters across the handlebars. Word got around fast. Big Davey complained to the principal, but the damage had already been done. Pete didn't have to worry about Davey anymore.

"My point is," Sean says, hands in his pockets, "if no one else is going to help, *we* gotta step in. Isn't that what Pa's been doing for as long as we can remember?"

I glance at Sean again. He makes me proud all over to be his brother, but he also makes me feel like a "yellow-bellied coward," just as John Wayne would call it, for wanting Sean to stay home.

And yet, as I listen to Sean, something stirs in me. The same thing that *always* happens. That familiar pull to be brave like him. To stand next to him in the hard places.

"Mikey," he says, gentle-like. "You and me, we're a team. There ain't nothing we can't face. But I *can't* sit by and do nothing, not with this injustice going on in the world. Not even if it's across the ocean, happening to people I don't know. If I join now, I'll get to *choose* where I serve."

I swallow hard. "What will I do when you leave, Sean?"

He nods, aware of my thoughts, and places his hand on my back. "You'll take care of Ma and Pa. You'll finish school. And you'll send me lots of letters. Especially about... oh, what's her name? Shelby?"

I freeze. My mouth hangs open, but nothing of substance comes out. I have *never* mentioned Shelby to Sean. He notices everything!

I punch his arm, grinning despite myself.

He laughs and messes up my hair with his hand. "Ah, knock it off, Sean, I'm too old for that."

"Never too old to be my younger brother!" He winks and chuckles, flashing the smile that puts the world right.

XV.

Scotland - 1945

Two days later, I find myself walking past a painted wooden sign that reads *Doomfrys*. It's a small city with an old-world charm, more like a village tucked away from time.

Dog and I didn't eat much yesterday; most of the day was spent coaxing him to keep moving. I like to get at least one square meal per day, so as I step onto the cobbled main street, I scan for a pub or cafe.

Few people wander the street. It's quieter than I expected. A man passes me, then a woman, both preoccupied, eyes downcast, as if their thoughts weigh heavier than their footsteps.

I soon come upon a swinging wooden sign for *The Globe Inn and Pub* and step inside. One man stands behind the bar, gruff and red-faced, and another sits at a table near the door.

The man at the table wears an older-style suit, nicely cut, and sports a thick mustache. He pushes his fork around the plate in slow, clockwise circles, not eating. His head stays bowed, so I can't see his face, but the whole place feels melancholy, trodden down.

60

"Are you serving meals?" I call to the man behind the bar.

He looks up and meets my eyes. I'm surprised to find that what I took for gruffness is softer, kinder than I first thought.

"Aye, Laddy," he says, rough-voiced but not off-putting. "I see you're hungry. I can get you a bit of toast and some stewed meat, but that's the best for today."

He must see weariness etched on my face, enough to know I need more than just a hot meal. I silently vow to find a place for a bath. It's been too many days since a shower, and weeks since I've looked at myself beyond the small shaving mirror in my travel kit.

"Thank you, sir. That would be great." I say.

He nods. "You'll have to take it outside. I'm closing soon for a wake."

"No problem. Sorry for your loss, sir."

"Thank you kindly. It is a sore loss." The pub owner glances sideways at the man by the door. "It didn't need to happen to such a young man," he adds loudly.

I follow his glance to the man at the table.

"Now, Jack! Say it outright if you mean to blame me like the rest of the village!" The thin, wiry man snaps upright, pounding his hand on the table.

With a humph and a grunt, Jack turns away and begins to prepare my meal.

"You've come on a black day, son. We're usually quite a friendly lot in Doomfrys," the seated man says, his face apologetic for the outburst.

"That's true, lad. That's the one thing he *is* right about," Jack calls over his shoulder. "But today, the whole town will be attending poor wee James McFarland's wake. Not much spirit left to socialize when you've lost a boy of only eighteen."

"The war?" I ask.

"Nay. We saved him from that peril, only to lose him to another." Jack wipes his hands on a towel, then sighs. "I've got to go now, sonny. *Banker Walsh* can tell you the rest; he knows the whole story." He sends another dark look toward the mustached man.

"Here's your food." Jack hands me a plate heaped with warm steaming meat and bread, then follows me out the front door.

"Just leave the plate by the door when you're done. I'll get it when I return. Here's a bowl of water for your dog."

Walsh, the banker, must've slipped out just before me. He lingers nearby, not quite leaving, as if waiting for something, perhaps me.

I sit next to the door and begin eating. Dog, grateful for the water, laps it up noisily, then lifts his head, still drooling, and sits on his hind legs, waiting patiently for me to share. I tear the bread, add a chunk of meat, and feed it to him.

The banker saunters back and forth, having nowhere else to go, apparently. Jack, the pub owner, walks briskly around the bend until he disappears.

"It's not my fault, I tell you."

The voice startles me. I looked up to see Walsh standing just a few feet away, staring down the road rather than at me. He lights a cigarette, takes two sharp puffs, then flicks it to the ground and crushes it underfoot. Without pause, he pulls out another and lights it. "No, sir," I say, not sure what I'm stepping into.

"They all want to blame me," he mutters. Then louder, "but I don't believe in ghost stories!"

Now he turns and looks directly at me. "You're American. So, you wouldn't know about all the old demons and spirits that folks around here still believe haunt the castles and moors."

My head snaps up. "Ghosts? Castles?" I ask.

"Maybe it'd be easier if I start from the top," Walsh says. "You don't mind, do you? It's a sad day, whether they let me attend the funeral or not. It'd be nice to talk with someone, better than being alone."

I'm not sure if I want to spend time chatting, as it's not my nature to make casual conversation. But there's a restless stirring inside me, the same feeling that's kept me moving for weeks.

"I can listen," I say.

"Well, you see, I *am* a banker," Walsh begins. "Born here, raised just two hills over. But I attended university in London, and they've never quite forgiven me for it."

He glances at me, gauging my attention, then continues.

"I deal in properties and inheritances. There's a very old castle here, built sometime in the 13th century. The townsfolk say it's haunted, cursed, and other such rot. Now, ye hear me," he points a finger at the air, "it's just a building, that's all, stone and mortar."

He exhales hard, and I wonder who he's trying to convince, me or himself.

"Well, the thing is, it's slowly wasting away. No one will care for it. Most won't even walk within a mile of the place!"

My gut twitches. He's talking about Doomfrys.

"It's my idea to help this town. Shops are shuttering left and right, and you've seen it; the square's nearly dead. So, I thought to meself, try and preserve the castle, not only for historical reasons, but to share it with tourists. Well, tourists like you," he points at me. "We need tourism. But the townsfolk? They're short-sighted, too caught up in old ways and ancient tales of bad blood to see the opportunity."

"I see…"

"But that isn't the worst of my problems. The town will come around, I believe that. No, the real issue is this: every time I hire workers to start some project on the castle property, they promptly quit. Some don't even make it through the gate!"

He stops abruptly and looks at me again. "Didn't catch your name?"

"Michael Cornell, sir. You're talking about Doomfrys Castle?" The question slips out before I even realize I've thought it.

"Nice to meet you, Michael," he says, dipping his head. "Yes, that's the one."

He shifts his weight, and his gaze lingers on the empty road. "In hopes of pushing this town past its paranoid, haunted notions about the castle, I offered a challenge. It was meant to be good fun. I'm trying to *help this town,* after all!"

Walsh looks down and kicks a loose stone in the road, frustration and rejection written in the movement.

"Yes," he continues, with little prompting from me. "So, I offered an incentive. Anyone willing to stay one full night in the castle earns a hundred pounds! A hundred pounds, Mikey! That's real money in post-war Scotland!"

I bristle at being called "Mikey" by a stranger, but I know it's just their way here.

"I figured if someone stayed the night and lived to laugh about it, we could finally put the ghost stories to rest, move past the nonsense, and begin renovations. Tourist revenue, preservation, it's all in the name of saving a special landmark, you see!"

"Makes sense." I throw in.

"I'm part of the Historical Heritage Society of Scotland, after all!" Walsh says a bit too defensively. "But no one here wants the castle tampered with. They say there's a wicked spirit lurking about the place. They want it left alone. It's bad luck to disturb such ground, they say."

He shakes his head, but his voice falters just a touch. "Maybe I should've listened in hindsight, but I still don't believe in ghosts or demons. Not really. Even after the, um, unfortunate result."

"So, this boy, James," I say, nudging him gently. "That's his name, right? Did he take up your challenge?"

"Yes. James McFarland," Walsh's voice softens. "A good lad. Full of bravado, maybe too much. Heard about the offer and came straight to me. Said he wanted the money to start a life with his sweetheart." He pauses, rubbing his chin, lost in the memory.

"So, I gave him the key, and off he went, head high, eager like. A few of his mates tagged along, said they'd split the money. They made a game out of it."

Walsh takes a deep breath and lights another cigarette. I sense we are approaching the heart of the story. Dog eyes him for a moment, but with the food gone loses interest, and rests his head on my thigh and begins to drift off.

"Well," Walsh begins, exhaling smoke slowly, "we didn't hear nothin' that night. I went up to the castle the next morning, expecting to see James's grinning face, holding out his hand for the hundred pounds."

Walsh's voice waivers, and he clears his throat. "But instead, just inside the doorway, in an old armchair, sat James. Rigid. Eyes wide. Face etched eternally with fright. His fingernails clawed deep into the wooden armrests."

I lean back against the pub wall, realizing I'd been leaning toward Walsh.

"Turns out his mates chickened out around midnight and left him there alone." He rubs his temples. "The doctor says it must've been a heart attack. But the whole town says that he was scared to death. *Literally, scared to death!*"

His voice drops. "Eighteen-year-olds don't just die of heart attacks, they say, despite what the doctor said. So now, they blame me. Poor wee Laddy, James McFarland! I expect his imagination ran wild and got the better of him. Got himself worked up. That kind of fear can do things to the body, you know. But it is true, like the doc says, a heart attack can happen to anyone, even the young. It's not my fault."

"And for that, you're not invited to the wake?" I try to sound sympathetic, but it comes out more like pity.

"Aye."

I study the wiry man before me. He's trying to stay composed, but it's clear he's burdened with guilt. Thinks it's partly his fault. The way he grips his cigarette like it might float away, the way he keeps muttering "Not my fault" under his breath, they give him away. And maybe he's right, to some degree, I can agree to that. Spirits didn't kill that boy. Surely there's some other explanation.

Still, one hundred pounds could go far in my travels. I have money of my own, but it's harder to access overseas. I don't *need* the cash, but I'm starting to miss home. Having funds in hand might make it easier to get back to the States when the time comes.

Besides, what's one night in an old castle compared to the nights I've survived? I've slept in foxholes under shellfire, where comrades were blown to bits before my eyes. I've already faced demons, and they were made of flesh and blood. A crumbling castle doesn't seem all that frightening in comparison.

I trust my instincts, and I wouldn't be alone. I've got Dog. I glance down at him, peacefully asleep, chin on my leg, tail twitching at some distant dream.

Maybe I'd be helping Walsh out, too. It must be a heavy thing to carry, the blame of a whole town for a beloved boy's death, true or not.

Most of all, if I'm honest with myself, I can't deny the pull of curiosity. The other reasons are justifications; I need to see that castle in person. I'm different from the townspeople. I don't put much stock in curses and bogeymen hogwash. Superstition is easy when you haven't lived through real monstrosities.

The words escape me before my mind can catch up. "Would you give me a shot at that deal, Mr. Walsh?"

He turns quickly, eyes narrowing as he sizes me up. "Really? A Yank? So, you're not fazed by our folk tales of restless souls?"

"No, sir. Seen worse on the battlefield, I'm guessing. Could use the cash, and I'm dependable. I know how to take care of myself."

He raises an eyebrow. "But you're barely older than poor wee James."

I'm chuffed. Surely the war has carved the boy out of me, rubbed the teenage shine off me. I feel forty, at least.

"Sir, I'm nearly twenty-five," I reply, steady. "And besides, no one in this town knows me. If something were to happen, it wouldn't stir half the grief James's death has. It won't hurt your standing more than it already has. And if all goes well, it'll help you out when I can testify that the castle is just a nice old pile of brick and mortar, good for a quiet night's rest."

That last line pulls a faint smile from Walsh's thin lips at the use of his own words.

As I speak, an image flickers through my mind: those two men standing by the castle in my dream. One calm. One hateful. What am I doing? Surely that dream *meant something,* a sign. What if it was a warning?

But it feels like destiny. I'm supposed to do this.

This strange pull to the north has been with me for weeks now. And here I am, trying to talk a man into letting me sleep in a castle where a boy died just nights ago. Never would've guessed my day would play out like this.

Mr. Walsh is still watching me, skeptical but thoughtful. I don't retract my offer. Somehow, in a way I can't explain, this feels like a step toward something I lost in the war. Courage? Purpose? Maybe it's that part of me that still needs to prove something, even after everything.

"Hmmm," Walsh murmurs, flicking his cigarette butt. "Very well said, soldier. But you'd need to promise not to come limping in, blaming me for a twisted ankle, or running wild, screaming about apparitions in the night!"

"No, sir," I reply. "I'm a man of my word. If I say I'll do it, I will."

He holds my gaze one last time, long enough to decide what kind of man he thinks I am.

"I believe you," he says, finally, nodding. "All right then, no time like the present. Come with me to the bank. I'll need you to sign a waiver, and then I'll give you the key."

XVI.

After picking up the castle key from the banker, I set off towards the old place. The key is ancient, thick iron, and heavy in my hands. Much too large and awkward to sit comfortably in a pocket. It feels more like a weapon than a door key.

As I walk, the metal begins to warm, absorbing the heat of my palm and radiating it back, almost as if it's alive. I push the thought aside.

A few townsfolk had words for me when they caught wind of what I was doing. I guess word travels fast in these small towns. Most stopped short of forbidding me, but their wide eyes and muttered warnings spoke louder than their words. I don't put much stock in their superstitions, but I'd be lying if I said their nervous energy hadn't rubbed off on me, just a little.

Even still, I'd rather arrive at the castle in daylight, see what I am up against. Best to understand what I'm dealing with before shadows start playing tricks.

My instructions were to keep to the road that runs alongside the River Nith, so I begin my walk. The land is surprisingly beautiful, sweeping flatlands and tall grass, interrupted now and then by rises of hillocks, like spines rising from the ground.

I keep my eyes on the road ahead, but the steady crunch of wheels soon draws my attention.

"Dog," I murmur, moving us to the side.

A wagon lumbers closer, pulled by a weary horse. The wooden wheels groan against the gravel, their rhythm echoing across the quiet fields. As the farmer nears, I lift a hand in greeting.

"Good day," I call.

To my surprise, he reins the horse in, halting the cart. "Where you headed, Yank?"

It still jars me, how quickly I'm marked as American, despite my efforts to blend in, as if the word's scrawled across my forehead. Then again, my boots, the pack slung across my shoulders, every piece of me shouts U.S. Military, so why am I surprised?

"To Doomfrys Castle, sir," I answer.

The man lets out a long, low whistle through weathered lips. "Nothing good ever came of that place," he mutters. "You certain that's where you want to go?"

"Yes, sir. I've been told it's not too far a walk."

The farmer looks to be pushing seventy. Deep lines crease his brow and gather at the corners of his eyes. A flat cap sits low on his head, while thick tufts jut out behind his ears. I suspect he's bald on top.

"If you're resolute, Laddy," he says at last. "I'll carry you near the castle grounds. But no closer."

Grateful for the offer, I nod and heave my duffel into the back of the hay wagon, and Dog leaps in after, shadowing my every move. He circles the hay a few times before curling into a ball, settling in.

We ride in silence for a stretch. The old man holds the reins loose in one hand, scratching idly at his knee. But it's plain enough to tell he's internally itching against something he wants to say. When he can't hold it in any longer, he scratches that itch and meets my eyes.

"You're not from around here," he begins, voice low and measured. "But my family's lived on this land for generations. You'll think us touched in the head, I expect. But some things, some things that go unexplained, are nonetheless real."

He gives a brief, grave nod, as if sealing his own words. "If ye are willing to listen, I ask only that ye hear me out. 'Tis my duty as an old father and a grandfather, meself."

"Yes, sir," I say, my tone still carrying the reflex of a soldier. "I'm listening."

The farmer nods again, taps his knee twice, then, like a wise grandfather indeed, he warns, "That castle you're headed for, it's an evil place. It's been cursed. Mark my words. I reckon that awful banker only gave you half the story."

"He told me about the young man who died there recently, yes."

"Aye, young James." His jaw tightens, and for a long moment, he says nothing. The sounds of life fill the air: the creak of the wagon and the steady clop of the horse, and cheerful birds chirping back and forth.

"Of course, he told you that. Spoke from guilt, no doubt. But not guilty enough to mention hundreds of years of death, darkness, and *foreboding* that came before."

I almost laugh at the emphasis he puts on *foreboding,* but when his eyes lock with mine, I see he's deadly serious. I cannot laugh at that. What happened in this town to make such grim beliefs cling so tightly?

"Sir, I appreciate your care. What do I need to know?"

He stops fussing at his leg and takes the reins in both hands, gripping them firmly, as if he needs something solid to hold while telling the tale.

"James wasn't the first," he says at last, his voice lowered, as if he's afraid some unseen force is listening. "This death wasn't the first. There have been many others. Strange things. But this story starts hundreds of years ago."

I lean in, eager for the history behind the place.

"Two brothers once lived in that castle, sons of a great Chieftain. The Doomfrys line guarded this valley, watched over that river." He nods towards the slow-moving water beside us. "But peace was broken. One brother killed the other. Right there, in that very castle. The ultimate betrayal."

Two brothers, I think to myself, *two men standing before the castle in my dream.*

"You see," he draws a long breath. "The elder brother was only a man, mind you, but a good one. A kind leader. The younger one, though, was a creature of envy. Selfish. Greedy. An angry fellow. Coveting his brother's position, he drove a blade into his chest. Yet the elder brother lived long enough to speak the truth. When the clan heard of the treacherous act, they dragged the younger brother to the north tower, where he was tortured and killed. But not before he spewed curses on the castle, the land, and the people."

He points in the direction ahead. "We don't take dark curses lightly around here, especially when cast upon your own kin. And that tower, the north tower, represents cursed souls and bloody death. All who cross the threshold are claimed. Stay away, young man."

My stomach knots as the farmer's voice sinks lower, thick with superstition. Yet beneath it, I hear sorrow too, as if he speaks of his own sons, like the grief carries through his generations.

My mind feels heavy with thought. I measure my instincts against the weight of a grown man's grim conviction. Maybe I've been too confident. Too quick to dismiss what the locals claim they've seen with their own eyes.

I shrug at the indescribable feelings, steeling myself. I force reason and logic to steady me. But in consideration of his words, and unbidden to my mind, the visions return. I see two men, brothers now in my mind. One with eyes bulging in terror. The other, with clawed, inhuman fingers wrapped tight around his throat, choking and killing.

I shove the image down, but like a thick fog over the moors, it refuses to clear.

"You see," the farmer presses on, "many say they catch glimpses of that younger brother still, wandering the castle grounds, pounding at the doors as if he's still desperate to be let back in. Others swear he stalks the moors in ghostly form, cursed to haunt the land."

He gestures toward the shadowed hills, his eyes dark. " They never buried him, you know. Left him to the wolves, somewhere out there. His guilty soul and blackened heart cannot rest. They say he moans in agony."

My mouth twitches, though I don't mean it to.

The old man fixes me with a hard look. "Don't laugh, Yank, I've heard it meself, out on the moors at dusk. This is nae a fairy story."

I wasn't about to laugh. The old man is too sincere, too worthy of respect, and his words are already sinking like a stone in my chest.

"But what of the older brother?" I ask, shifting uneasily on the wagon seat.

"He lies in peace, hopefully," the farmer says. "Buried in the family graveyard at Doomfrys. No one sees *him*. He was a good man, no doubt at rest. But…" he adds, lowering his voice again, "some whisper he *can't* rest. Not fully. Not until he has been avenged. Some say he's locked in the north tower still, waiting to be released. Waiting, watching. Trapped until justice is done."

The farmer glances into the distance toward the dark, hulking silhouette rising from the moors. "We're getting closer. Not too much longer now."

"But wasn't justice served when the younger brother was killed for his crime?" I ask, more invested in the story than I'd like.

"Well, nae, sonny," he says slowly, "You don't know our ways. Stubborn, the clans were. The younger brother's betrayal ruined the family for many years to come. The Chieftain Doomfrys died from a broken heart, and the clan scattered. See, there was no true justice for them."

"I see," I murmur, as if it makes perfect sense.

"And in case that isn't enough to trouble you," the farmer adds, leaning forward on the reins, "here's more for you to stew on. For fifty years now, folks round here have heard wolves crying in the night, a dreadful howling. Not one or two, mind you, a whole pack. The howls come from the castle itself, like they're circling it. Hunting."

"Why is that strange?" I ask, glancing instinctively over my shoulder at the mention of wolves, just to confirm Dog still rests in the back of the wagon.

"Strange indeed, Laddy," he says grimly. "Mark my words, there haven't been wolves in all of England or Scotland for hundreds of years."

The hairs on my neck prickle, and sharp ice jolts through my body. I sit up straighter, roll my shoulders, and try to shake the sensation. *Folklore. Old wives' tales.*

Every old town has its legends. Scotland thrives on them, loch monsters, banshees, and faerie rings. Wolves circling ghost-haunted castles? No different than the *beast in the woods* back home, or the tales my friends spun around campfires.

And really, what could be worse than what I've already witnessed on the battlefield? If grisly, bloody death called spirits, then the trenches of France should have been choking with the haunting of them every night.

"You're not the first tourist to meddle with that place," he continues. "People've gone missing around here for years. Just a decade ago, a salesman came to town. He went from farm to farm, house to house, you know, a tinker. Sold pots and pans, mended metal, and sharpened knives. Not much business around here, but he lingered. Quiet fellow. Kept to himself. One morning, a few of us saw him walking toward the castle, said he had an appointment at the farmhouse beyond. He never showed. His bags stayed at the inn. Never claimed."

Another pause. Each one falling heavier than the last. The old man's stories piling on like earth thrown onto a coffin, slow, deliberate, and foreboding.

The brown mare labored up the slight incline. I focus on the clop, clop, of each hoof.

"Most recently, a young lass was found drowned in this very river, right by the castle," the farmer says, pointing to the dark river, swirling in chaos.

"Her dress torn; body wrapped in reeds. Many claim a demon's hand did it." At that, the farmer turned to look at me, searching my face for disbelief or fear. I hold his gaze without flinching.

Certain I'm not swayed, he presses on.

"There was also a group of workmen," he continues. "That banker sent them over. Every single one of them came back swearing their tools were cursed. Couldn't hit a nail straight, no matter how hard they tried. They'd set down a saw only to have it vanish while their backs were turned." He clicks his tongue for emphasis.

"The foreman stayed behind one evening to finish some fencing near the boundary lines. The next morning, they found him slumped in the grass, unconscious. Two black eyes, nearly swollen shut. He doesn't remember a thing and refuses to speak of it. But he made one thing clear: none of his men would ever return to that property." I give no reply, only listen. My silence seems to frustrate him, and he lets out a short huff through his nose, begrudgingly accepting it. Moments pass.

"Well, I tried to warn ye. There it is," the farmer says. "Right up there around this bend, you'll get your first view of the castle."

He points with his elbow, not letting go of the reins, as if his life depends on gripping them tight.

From all the stories I've now heard, I expected the castle to be larger. I pictured a fortress with a proverbial storm cloud hanging over it. The black-and-white photo in the library created an intensity, amplified the structure into a considerable size, and a menace in my mind.

Instead, I see a weathered building of heavy stone. The infamous north tower rises solemnly to one side, balanced by a matching tower on the south. It is a castle, yes, but time has wrapped it in neglect.

Shrubs, brambles, and low trees have overrun the base of the castle, their roots and branches tangled in such a way that they have become one, as if the land itself is reclaiming the structure, inch by inch, dragging it deeper into the unknown.

The wagon rolls closer, and more details emerge. A long, rocky drive stretches toward the front entrance. Narrow windows, too small to let in much light, peer out from the walls, and weathered turrets jet skyward.

The sun dips low, casting a soft amber glow across the castle, but the golden light offers no warmth, nor comfort.

Suddenly, the wagon jolts and lurches to a stop, perpendicular to the drive of Doomfrys. The farmer stares straight ahead, focused on the road, refusing to look at the place.

I want to acknowledge his warning, to show respect for his concerns, but no words come, so I remain stoic.

The farmer tilts his head and studies me one last time, wizened eyes narrowing. "Laddy," he says, voice low, "I haven't changed your mind. I can see it plain as day. But heaven won't hold *me* accountable for what happens to ye. I've done my part, and I've warned ye."

"No, sir," I reply evenly. "You're free from any blame. I take your words to heart, and I'll take care."

A pang of guilt strikes me. We are mutually disappointed. He hasn't convinced me to turn back, and I left him unsettled, uncomfortable, and only stirred up dread for him.

I mutter, "Thank you."

The road ahead of him stretches along, hugging the river; going on for miles, and the farmer's fingers twitch; he's anxious to be moving on.

78

"I'll let you off here, then," he says. "I go no closer to that abomination."

"Yes, sir."

I jump down from the seat, boots crunching on the gravel.

"Dog."

Dog rises from his bed of hay, shakes, and jumps from the wagon to my side. I sling my duffel over my shoulder and turn toward the castle. When I glance back, the wagon is already pulling away.

"I'd keep that dog near ye," the old man calls over his shoulder. "House pets go missing around here."

I barely catch the last few words. Before I can reply or thank him again, he lifts a hand above his head, not turning. A farewell, perhaps, or a silent washing of his hands free of me, and of whatever comes next.

XVII.

The dirt drive is narrow and long, flanked by tall, slender trees whose overgrown branches lean inward, forming a tunnel that grows darker the farther I walk.

Being late in the afternoon, the canopy of overgrowth blocks out the sun so thoroughly that it feels as though I've stepped indoors. The tunnel's closeness presses in, confining and eerie.

Far ahead, the castle looms, a silhouette against the dimming sky, its towers etched by the setting sun. Dusk is settling in. With my duffel bag slung over my shoulder, I take a few steps, then stop. Dog isn't following.

"Come on, Dog," I call.

He's rigid, ears pricked, nose twitching. Watching.

"Dog," I repeat, firmer this time.

Slowly, reluctantly, he rises and follows me into the narrowing dark. The path behind him seems to close tighter once he passes beneath the branches, like a hallway swallowing him whole.

I exhale and mutter out loud, *"Even the dog's getting superstitious."*

I'm grateful for the farmer's hospitality, warnings, and all. If I'd walked the distance on foot, the sun would have vanished long before I reached Doomfrys' gates.

I realize, as I near the castle, that it's too quiet. Unnaturally so. The trees lining the drive seem to muffle even my footsteps. Silence.

I study the trees, trying to place them, but nothing about them looks familiar. Their bark is smooth and pale, the limbs almost unnervingly symmetrical. Wrong, somehow. I step closer to inspect one, and that's when I see them. Low, white-flowering bushes twined around the trunks like long-fingered hands wrapped around a neck. It's Hemlock. I'd know it anywhere.

I take an instinctive step back. *Leave that alone,* my mind whispers. A brief, dusty memory breaks through. Sean's face flashes before me.

"Danger, Mikey!" he shouts, urgent and vivid, as if he's right beside me.

Shaken, I call Dog closer. He obeys.

More silence. No birds, nothing.

I drag my eyes away from the trees and look down the path. Squinting, I see something. Or someone? I can't tell yet, so I slow my pace. Dog's growl vibrates low against my leg as he presses close.

A breeze sweeps through the tunnel, rustling leaves and carrying a breath of chill. I can't tell if it's the moving air or the strange stillness clinging to the place, but suddenly, I feel cold. A slight shiver quakes my body, and I keep moving.

Closer now, I see something, or someone, leaning against a tree on my right. At first, it looks like a very short man, or maybe some kind of animal. The posture is wrong, strange, and I can't make out the form.

I keep walking, but instinct urges me to quicken my pace. Projecting confidence in my steps, I walk tall as I draw near the figure.

The unknown entity, I realize, is not short, but rather hunched. Huddled low, crouched almost on all fours. *Just a man,* I tell myself.

His clothes are in tatters, shredded remnants that might once have been a cloak, now nothing more than filth-streaked rags. His hair is long, gray, and matted, hanging in unkempt ropes over his shoulders. A thick beard obscures most of his face and neck. Dirt and grime coat him as though he's slept amongst the tree roots.

I take another step and can see his hands with long, yellowed fingernails curling like claws from cracked fingers. I raise my hand in reflex to greet him, but he turns. His eyes lock on mine, and I freeze.

Red-rimmed and wild, his gaze is sharp and feral and burns straight through me. My mind scrambles to make sense of this thing. Is it man or creature?

"Hello there," I call out, voice surprisingly steady

The creature responds, not with words, but with movement. It bends lower, collapsing fully onto all fours, limbs jerking at unnatural angles. Then the noises start, thick, guttural sounds, rising from deep in its throat, not quite human.

Dog erupts, barking, snarling, and then yelping, but remains at my side. He presses tight against my leg, trembling. I glance down. His tail is tucked between his legs, putting me on immediate alert.

Another foreboding wind whips through the tunnel-like trees, and Dog senses it too. Taking his lead, I know something is deeply, terribly wrong here.

82

No longer interested in seeing what happens next, I break into a full run. The trees blur past, but instead of opening, the path feels narrower, the forest is shrinking, folding in around us, closing in on us with every step. The castle door, once within reach, feels farther away.

But I know I'm moving, and logically, I am getting closer. I keep pumping my legs. Dog stays at my side; he doesn't run ahead, his paws pounding the earth to keep pace with me. I reach the base of the castle steps and take them three at a time. Dog is on my heels.

I fumble for the ancient key, the one that barely fits in my pocket, that Walsh gave me, and jam it into the lock. Behind me, I hear the creature hit the stairs, fast. I risk a glance.

It's bounding after me, foam flinging from its rabid mouth in thick strands, limbs pumping with inhuman speed.

Dog barks furiously but doesn't intercept, surprisingly he doesn't take the defensive with this anomaly. Even he knows it's beyond instinct or training.

I put pressure on the key, but it won't turn. I shove harder, but it refuses to turn. I try again, and again. It won't turn! *Wrong key?* For a panicked split second, I curse the banker for giving me the wrong one.

The creature is nearly on me; the beast has reached the top of the stairs. Desperate, I twist the key the other direction.

Click. It turns.

In one motion, I kick Dog inside, dive through after him, and hurl my duffel to the ground. Just as the creature lunges, I slam the heavy door shut in its vicious, snarling face.

The impact nearly knocks me back. It slams against the other side, hard. Wild howls, guttural and pained, penetrate through the wood and echo violently in the entryway. Outside, claws rake, nails tear, furious scrapes gouge across the surface. A series of dull thuds, kicks, or fists pounds relentlessly on the door. The entire frame shutters.

I throw my weight against the door, heart thundering. My hand scrambles along the wall until I find it: a wide plank of old wood, maybe six inches thick, four feet long. A door bar.

I lift it, slot it into the iron brackets bolted into the frame, and slam it down. Secured. I step away, just one pace, then whip around, eyes locked on the door. It's still braced. Still trembling. Breathe. Breathe.

My training kicks in. I control my breath. I let the adrenaline slow, then ebb completely. The pounding fades, the scratching weakens. The howls retreat, becoming fainter and drifting into the distance.

The castle falls silent, just as cold and still as the tree-lined tunnel I ran through. Dog huddles between my legs. I pull him closer, feeling the tremor in his body match my own.

XVIII.

Europe – 1942

Sean is dead. I hold his last letter in one hand, and in the other, the one from my parents. They've left the formal telegram attached, including the president's *"deepest regrets,"* a notice informing them that their firstborn died in a country I can't even point to on a map.

WESTERN UNION

31 GOVT
WASHINGTON D C 845PM 11-18-42 CALVIN & LILLIAN CORNELL

THE SECRETARY OF WAR DESIRES ME TO EXPRESS HIS DEEPEST REGRETS THAT YOUR SON CORPORAL SEAN C. CORNELL WAS KILLED IN ACTION ON FOURTEENTH NOVEMBER IN NORTH AFRICA, FRENCH MOROCCO

LT GENERAL D EISENHOWER

In Sean's final letter to me, just weeks earlier, he wrote of his band of brothers, the men he served with, and reassured me he was honored to call me his *real* brother, too. *"Proud of my brave kid-brother, an air-trooper, no less. Showing me up already."*

But it was the last lines that burned into my soul:

"Mikey, some fights are worth the cost, and this one is. One day soon, you and I will meet on our favorite rock when it's all over."

A few months later, another letter arrived, this one from Aunt Geraldine. Mama and Pa were gone, too. *Influenza. Fast. Unexpected.* Gone.

XIX.

Scotland - 1945

Feeling safer with the creature barred outside, I finally allow myself to take in my surroundings. The castle interior is dim, lit only by the last rays of the setting sun slipping through narrow cracks in the stone.

I pull the drawstrings and unhook the clasp on my duffel and extract my flashlight, and for good measure, I pocket a small box of matches too.

I click on my flashlight, and the beams cut through the shadows, revealing a vast, open vestibule. Straight ahead, a heavy wooden door hangs slightly ajar, leading to another room swallowed in darkness.

To my immediate right, a stone spiral staircase winds upward, which is presumably the north tower. An identical set curls up to the left: the south tower. Beneath each staircase, arched passageways open into deeper chambers beyond.

I recall what the townspeople said, the story about the young man, James. Found dead, stiff in this very entry. My flashlight lands on an old wooden chair nearby, with a high, carved back looming as a testifier. The patterned fabric on the seat is worn through.

I can picture him clearly: James, collapsing in horror, knuckles white on the armrests, mouth open in a scream no one heard. The expression mirrors the disbelief I've seen on the faces of dozens of men in war-torn France. Disbelief that this was how they would die. Scared and stunned at the sudden, unrelenting grip of death.

But a heart attack in such a young man? Maybe his experience on the road was like mine. Maybe he saw the same creature I did. Or worse. Possibly, he didn't make it past that chair.

Still, I feel a flicker of confidence. I've faced battle. I've run for my life under enemy fire after dropping into hostile territory. The war seems worse than this castle, and I've survived far worse.

At least, that's what I tell myself.

I decide to get my bearings by walking the castle end to end. Knowing the layout will help me feel more in command and give me an idea of the best place to spend the night.

I choose to explore the room straight ahead, not particularly eager to go up either of the staircases yet. Dog stays glued to my side. I feel pity for him and allow him to pad along underfoot.

The door pushes open with relative ease, and it appears to have once been a library or study. A large window overlooks the back gardens, now choked by weeds and tangled overgrowth. In the dusk light, it's easy to tell that the grounds were once beautiful and well-tended. Now, the wild and chaotic, twisted vines, are left to fend for themselves, completely abandoned. Still, I note that the moonlight will reach through this window. That could be useful later.

There's a worn armchair in the room and a massive fireplace. A few ancient candelabras still perch on the mantel, coated in dust. The room is empty of life, but not the echoes of memory. Like the rest of the castle, it's bare of furnishings but has a few scattered remnants here and there, as though it had been stripped hastily and then forgotten. Every room I enter carries the same weight: damp, cold, and oppressively lonely.

"That banker has his work cut out for him," I say to Dog. The other ground floor rooms prove to be old bed chambers, a large sitting room, and a once grand dining hall. The silence is constant, except for the sound of my boots and Dog's quiet pads on the stone.

Eventually, a narrow and steep staircase takes me down to the kitchens. The air is even colder, with the faintest scent of long-dead ashes. Massive fireplaces line the walls, blackened from centuries of use. Rusted cooking grates and chipped crockery lay scattered about. It must have been a bustling place in its time, servants rushing up and down those steps with bread, meat, and soup sloshing in heavy bowls. Feeding a clan would have been a never-ending job for the women. It must have been exhausting.

I do not envy them, working in a confined, smoky basement like this. I spot a door near the back, likely leading outside. I right an overturned worktable and drag it in front of the door. It won't stop anyone determined, but it might give me a few seconds' warning. I'm eager to leave this moldy place.

Only the towers remain unexplored. But the sun is nearly gone now, and I want to conserve my flashlight. I want to be settled.

From outside, I saw that both towers are high and well-fortified, surrounded by sheer stone walls. In the olden times, invaders wouldn't have been able to scale those impressive defenses, which means they are less of a concern to me right now. And, right now, I don't need elevation. I need security. The towers can wait.

All the rooms I've explored have more than one door, hallways feeding into hallways, like a maze built for confusion. For this reason, I decide that the library, with a single entrance, will be the best option to hunker down. Easier to secure, easier to defend. From there, I can watch the garden through the window and have only one door to guard.

I return to the library and drag the large chair, like the one in the entryway, against the far wall next to the window. It's the best position, only a stone wall at my back–it's cold, but solid.

I shut the door and secure it from the inside, using an old iron latch and wedging a chunk of splintered wood beneath the handle. Then I strike a match and light the dusty candles in the candelabras, I set one on the floor beside my chair, and leave the other on the mantel, to illuminate the room. It casts long, flickering shadows across the confined space.

I switch off my flashlight. I may need the batteries later. The full moon has risen now, casting pale light over the wild garden. I try to imagine how it must've looked in its prime with tended paths, trimmed hedges, and flowers blooming in orderly rows. What it looked like when it was a cheerful place, before all the suspicion and stories, before Doomfrys Castle became a place of fear.

I dig through my duffel and pull out my .45, still wrapped in a shirt at the bottom. I load the magazine but leave the chamber empty. I sit down in the chair and place the gun in my lap, the flashlight on the armrest of the chair.

Dog curls at my feet, his body warm against my boots. He doesn't sleep, not really, but he's calm. And that's enough.

The light in the room grows briefly brighter and then dims again as clouds pass over the moon. Despite the cold dampness of the castle, I feel warm and secure where I am, but I won't sleep. I guess it's about 10 p.m. *This won't be too bad,* I tell myself. Just a night-watch. I've sat through many of those, in much worse circumstances.

I settle in for the night. Eyes fixed on the garden; ears alert to every sound.

XX.

My eyes flutter open. How could I let myself fall asleep? I don't know how much time has passed, but judging by the placement of the moon, now higher, and angling through the window, it must be around one or two in the morning.

What woke me?

The candles at my side have gone out. The room is darker, and the temperature has dropped to near frigid.

Dog is no longer curled at my feet, warm and still. He's standing, rigid and alert. His body blocks the space between me and the hearth.

I sense that he is ready to bark like mad. I reach out and place my hand on his back to calm him. His spine feels like coiled wire. His muscular frame is ready for action.

His gaze doesn't leave the hearth. I whisper his name, but he won't sit. Won't blink. Won't move. He's pointing. He's staring, signaling danger. But I see nothing, hear nothing.

"Dog, you're making me nervous. You're okay, boy. Lay down," I say, coaxing him to sit at least on his hind legs.

Then, as the moon slips behind a thick bank of clouds and the last of the light is swallowed whole, I feel it. A cold breeze brushes my cheeks and hands.

This makes no sense. The room is locked up solid. The library door is shut and barred. The windows are closed. There isn't a draft coming from the chimney; I imagine it's been blocked with leaves or animal nests over time.

Dog lets out a low, choked bark.

I fumble for the flashlight, knocking it off the armrest. My fingers scramble in the dark until I grip the cold metal and flick it on. I aim the beam towards the fireplace.

Empty. Nothing. Just soot and stone.

"Dog…" I whisper, more to myself than him. "Come, boy. Stay by me."

But no amount of coaxing will get Dog to be still, or to lie down. He won't even flick an ear at my voice.

My words contradict what he senses. He senses something I can't see. A shrill shiver runs up my spine. Hadn't I heard somewhere that animals can sense spirits? Demons?

I grit my teeth. Hogwash.

I must do better. No more sleeping. I'm shocked that I let myself doze off at all. It's this place, the heavy air is like a spell. My rest was troubled; some indistinct dream tugged at the edge of my mind, always out of reach. It's unsettling that I can't remember it, especially because it felt important.

I pull the matches from my pocket and light all the candles. The ones on the mantle are nearly spent, wax dripping thickly down their stems, but I leave them burning. I want the light.

I place the flashlight back on the chair's armrest. The candelabra beside me flickers, and our shadows, mine and Dog's, stretch and shift on the stone walls like silent watchers. It all feels looming. The walls seem to lean closer, the room shrinking, suffocating. *Watching me back.*

Just a few more hours till dawn, I tell myself over and over. We'll make it through this strange night. Then Dog and I can leave this place, collect the reward, and be done with it. Move on. Halfway home.

I rest the gun more securely across my lap. Another hour crawls by. Finally, Dog lowers himself into a sitting position beside me, but he won't lie down. His ears stay sharp and high, tracking every sound.

The air in the room suddenly feels strangely intoxicating, thick, and warm. It curls in my lungs and behind my eyes. Urging me to close my eyes for just a moment. I yawn. My body grows heavy, as if the very stones of the castle are pulling me deep down into them, inviting me to sleep. My fingers drift to Dog's head, stroking his fur softly...

XXI.

I wake again, this time jerking upright. Dog is growling, low and vicious, unrelenting. My hands and face register a familiar movement of air; it's stale, heavy, and wrong. It's more than a breeze. My brain snaps to instant alertness, panic slamming into my chest. My instincts take over.

The surging air blows out the candles. The sudden shift springs me upward. I knock the chair over, and my flashlight flies across the room. A discouraging shatter confirms it's broken. Useless. Darkness.

Luckily, I still grip the .45 in my hand.

I hear Dog charge toward the fireplace, his bark furious and wild. There's no light! No moon! I can't see a thing. I raise my gun, straining with only my ears to piece together what's happening.

We are no longer alone, I'm sure of it. Beastly snarls and deep savage growls rip through the darkness. They don't belong to Dog. These aren't human sounds either. They're pure hatred in sound form.

I swing my pistol towards the chaos, heart pounding. I don't dare to fire, not without eyes on Dog. I can't risk him.

"Dog!" I yell. "Come to me, boy!"

He doesn't come to me, and the fight continues. Overwhelming fear for him drowns everything out. I crouch, one hand braced on the ground, reaching blindly, trying to catch hold of him. But he's everywhere at once, twisting and thrashing as he wrestles in a frantic fight. I can't catch him.

The fighting escalates. Wood splinters, and I hear the sharp scrape of heavy paws scrambling, sliding across the floor.

I jam my hand into my pocket and claw out the box of matches. Adrenaline is making me clumsy. My fingers fumble for a single matchstick.

Dog lets out one final, high-pitched yelp.

Then silence.

I strike a match, but the air shifts again, and the brief flame is extinguished before it lights up the room. The draft vanishes. The room feels sealed once more. Tomb-like. I freeze.

My heart hammers wildly. Every instinct tells me *not* to move. But I force my body to obey. I must light the candles; surely, they are scattered across the floor. Or, maybe I can mend my flashlight. I *need* to see.

Either way, I want to do it quickly.

I strike a match, distressed to find that I only have a few left. A dim halo of flame lights the room for a few seconds, and in that glimpse, I see wreckage. My flashlight lies in pieces. The candles have rolled across the floor. Dust is disturbed everywhere, slashed and scattered by the struggle.

No Dog.

Near the fireplace, a dark, viscous pool spreads slowly outward. My throat clenches. It's Dog's blood.

I'm stunned. Confused. The match burns down rapidly and stings my fingers. I hiss and drop it. I've been staring at nothing for too long.

I stumble through the room, my breath coming in short bursts. I tell myself I've had worse. Panic won't help. But my body is on the edge of collapse. It's all crashing down on me now, the stories, the dream, the warnings from townsfolk. And Dog, gone.

Calm down, Cornell! Survive first, fall apart later. How many times had I barked those exact words to my unit? When soldiers dropped in mangled piles around us, and I had to make, even coax, the men to move forward.

I strike another match, this time leaning down and grabbing a candle. As I bring it closer to the flame, a flicker of movement catches my eye, outside the window. I blow out the match. I don't want whatever is out there to see me, not when I'm blind to it.

Moonlight filters through a break in the clouds, silver and faint. There, just at the edge of the garden, I see it. A figure crouched low to the ground, blanketed in darkness and brush. Two hundred feet away, the creature moves oddly, almost crawling, or floating.

It's carrying something across its back, but it is hard to tell what with the strange way it huddles so close to the ground when it walks. I strain my eyes and move closer to the window. I force my vision farther, squinting into the dark. The form becomes recognizable.

Dog. Limp and motionless. Slung across the creature's shoulders like a trophy.

Panic flares, fast and sharp. But then comes the second wave, hot, bitter fury. Rage. I slam my fist against the stone wall, feeling the sharp crack of skin and bone.

Dog depended on me! That scared, loyal animal. Hadn't he been through enough? Why did I bring him here? He trusted me. He protected me till the end.

"I'm counting on you," Sean's voice rings in my ears.

My throat and eyes burn from the smoky room, and my body shakes with the pain of losing Dog. If I weren't flooded with adrenaline, I'd shed tears. But anger leaves no room for that now.

I press my forehead to the cold glass, watching the silhouette grow smaller, moving farther into the blackened landscape. It drifts into the brush, beyond the far edge of the property, toward the wild moors.

And then it's gone.

I rub my bloodied fist, flexing my fingers through the sting. I stop myself mid-way from punching the wall again. I might need these hands before the night is over.

XXII.

There is nowhere to go. I don't feel safe anywhere now, not in this room, not in the towers, and not in the drafty halls echoing dark. Not outside with *that thing*. The farmer's warnings reverberate like a whisper in the back of my skull. *Don't go to the towers.* I won't. I can't.

I press my back against the wall, trying to focus. My military training claws its way to the surface. I need to think clearly and be ready for whatever comes next.

React. Reinforce. Recalibrate. Survive.

I snatch up the chair and inspect my flashlight. Shattered. Nothing left to save.

I gather what little light I have. A few candles remain, wax melted nearly to the base. Just a couple of inches of wax between me and total darkness. I light them all. I place the candelabra back on the mantle, but slide it to a new position, as if that will keep the flames alive. The flickering glow makes me twitch each time my shadow shifts on the wall.

I grip the .45 tightly and slip behind the chair, back to the wall for a shred of cover, or at least less vulnerability. It's not much, but no one, or no thing, can creep up behind me. It's the only barricade I have.

I stand there. Holding my breath.

Dog.

My throat tightens. I force myself to stop thinking of Dog, but I can't. He flashes before me anyway: ears alert, tail tucked, eyes wide with trust. Tears spring up, blurring my vision.

Stop it. Focus.

I close my eyes. Inhale slowly, exhale.

Creatures don't appear out of nowhere. Which means if it's here, it came from somewhere in this room.

***

Another hour drags by, though it feels like a painful lifetime. Sunrise must be less than two hours away now. The castle remains still with the same suffocating, predatory silence. My ears strain for any sound, but nothing comes. I keep my eyes fixed on the fireplace, every muscle tight, finger on the trigger.

In the distance, a great howling begins. *Wolves?* Or something worse? Are those screams coming from the tower? It's as if the castle itself, deep within its walls, howls in torment.

Hold it together. Just hold it together.

I held it together for three long years in war. I can hold it together in this room for two more hours. I have my wits. I have my gun.

But I'm realizing how quickly my seams are fraying, how near the edge I actually am. I wasn't whole when I entered this castle. My brain won't let me ignore that in the war, I knew who the enemy was. I knew *what* the enemy was.

This thing, this phantom, isn't just stalking me. It's inside my head, clawing at my mind, toying with my psyche. I must rein it in.

Then, for the third time, there's a shift in the air. My pistol rises on instinct, aimed at the fireplace. This time I'm ready.

The current sweeps past the candelabra and extinguishes the candles in a final sputter. In the dying glow, I glimpse it: a dark mass emerging from the hearth, blotting out what little light remains. It's growing bigger. Moving towards me.

This time, I snap. Suddenly it's all too much. My composure breaks. I do what I never did as a soldier; *I panic.*

The stories, the myths, the farmer's warnings, a brother's callous murder, a drowned girl in the river, James scared literally to death, it all floods me. Chokes me. This castle is evil and haunted. Alive. And my gun feels worthless, powerless in my hand. My irrational mind tells me bullets won't work.

Instead of firing, I roar in frustration and heave the chair toward the thing. The rushing creature stumbles, slipping through Dog's blood, and slams into the chair with a sickening thud.

I don't wait. I seize the moment and charge for the door. A wild thought flashes: *if the chair struck the creature, a bullet can too.* I twist, aim, and fire into the dark. The gunshot cracks like thunder in the chamber as I lift the bar and yank open the library door.

Behind me, the creature snarls, louder now, closer, gaining ground on me.

I sprint for the great front door, heart hammering, but I realize I'll never lift that massive bolt in time before it catches up. At the last second, I veer sharply towards the stairs. I tear upward, boots slipping on stone.

The North Tower!

A jolt of warning flashes in my brain. *No. Not the North Tower. The dream. Sean being strangled. Danger, Mikey!*

But it's too late. I'm trapped, running in circles, spiraling up the curved stairwell, stone walls squeezing in on all sides. Slivers of dawn bleed through arrow-slit windows, just a hint of light, my only hope.

Higher, higher I run. Angry growls follow close behind. At last, I reach the landing of the North Tower. A rush of icy wind from the open turret doorway hits my back as I spin around to face it.

The creature is only a few stairs below. I back into the room, mind racing, trying to think, trying to strategize, but the stench hits me first, rancid and stomach-turning. It slams against me like a brick wall.

Death. Rot. Decay so thick I taste it on my tongue. Rancid things, piled in corners, slumped against the walls. Rats? Animals? Bodies? I can't tell if it's real or if my fear is turning everything monstrous.

There's one more exit, a doorway that leads to the turret, a narrow balcony. I inch backward toward it, heart hammering. I'm out of options. My eyes stay locked on the snarling shape.

It enters the room. Not human in my eyes, just a mass of blood, filth, and violence. It laughs, a sound scraped from some gaping pit, mocking me with the castle's own voice, amused at my stupidity, as if luring me here, to the North Tower, was always the plan.

I step onto the balcony. Over the waist-high wall, the drop is dizzying. I wouldn't survive it. Sean's voice cuts through the panic, clear and sharp as if he's beside me.

"Courage," he says.

My mind flashes to James. The still-young man in the front entry. He didn't make it to dawn. Did he fight? Was he able to even try? Or did the tower take him too?

I'm a soldier. I'm not going out like this, damn it! This thing will not dictate my final moments! I didn't live through that bloody, horrifying war to have some demon orchestrate my death!

I am one sunrise away from ending this cursed night. After all I've endured, I realize I'm stronger than the last three years that tried to break me. Stronger than this creature. What's more, my gun is clenched tightly in my hand, a lifeline I refuse to let go of.

I stop retreating and stand my ground. Eyes locked. It abruptly halts as I face the creature. No running. No panic. I offer stillness, sanity, and an unwavering stare.

It's head jerks and thrashes. The mad laughter has mutated into snarls and guttural howls. White foam bubbles at the corners of its mouth, rabid growls spray thick spittle that clings to its matted, tangled beard. My stomach churns. I might vomit.

Its eyes flash with malice. Hate. I force myself to stare at the sharp yellow teeth and snarling lips. Swelling red circles around its eyes make it hard to tell if it's the creature's true eyes glowing red and bloodshot, or just the puffy, inflamed skin surrounding them.

It steps forward, one deliberate foot closer. I don't flinch. I hold my ground. I will not yield.

More snarling, more gnashing, more aggressive rage, but it doesn't move closer.

Then I notice the color beneath the madness: brown irises rimmed in yellowed, muddy whites. They are not the eyes of a beast. They are the eyes of a man, tortured, twisted, completely unmoored. I can't look away.

I step forward. Another slow step, and then another. Confidence rises, steadiness. Courage.

He backs away. Slowly, towards the steps.

I raise my gun and aim, projecting aggression to test him.

He recoils again, retreating down a few more stairs. I follow to the top of the landing.

"Move!" I shout, surprising even myself.

And then, in a split second, the twitch of a facial expression, the fleeting snarl of an enraged animal, dissolves, transforms into something else. His whole form shrinks, almost childlike. Is that... fear?

I blink. The hate is gone. The gnashing is gone. The foam no longer flies. I see him for what he is. I see not a monster, but a broken soul. A pitiful lunatic, crazed, exposed, and vulnerable. A mind torn beyond the brink. I've seen this look before, men worn down by too many battles, the weight of the fight.

His eyes, muddy, yellow, glassy, lock on mine. They seem to cry, *Why?* I hear the words in my mind. *"Don't hurt me,"* they plead. *"I'm weak. You are strong. Why are you doing this?"*

A high-pitched wail escapes his cracked lips. He trembles. I see a fragile old man, ruined by something too vast to name. But I keep the gun pointed. He continues his awful, agonized, pathetic whining, each step magnifying his torment.

As he retreats, his face contorted with increased agony, face twisted in raw, exposed suffering, staring at the gun aimed steadily at his body. It's the shaking that reminds me. Dog.

Dog's trembling body after the bomb blasts. His shattered courage. His warmth, his loyalty. I think of his weight curled against me in the foxhole. I think of Dog's broken spirit.

My grip on the pistol slackens. I lower it. My voice softens. "Let me help you," my voice croaks. I reach out my hand.

But just as quickly, the moment I do, he strikes. My lowered gun is a trap orchestrated by the creature.

The pleading face vanishes, transforms back into blazing, uncontrollable rage. He howls. The scream that rips from his throat is ancient, inhuman. It's a terrifying scream that shakes my soul.

His eyes blaze, truly ignited with red, burning fury.

He lunges, his clawed fingernails rake across my face, and I feel flesh tear. He grips my shoulders, trying to shove me back up the stairs.

I fight back. *I will not retreat.* I will not die in the North Tower. Despite his strength, I'm able to brace and push back. But he's fast and wild, all malevolence and madness.

The gun is knocked from my grasp. It clatters, tumbling down the stairs, out of reach.

I grab his bony shoulders, frail under the filthy rags, but he still has the advantage of momentum. He drives me back a step, and I almost fall. I plant my feet and thrust him away with every ounce of strength I have.

He stumbles backward and misses the step.

Time slows. Yet a new terror grips me as he slips and falls. His head smacks the tower wall with a sickening crack, then another as his skull hits a stone stair. Then another, and another. His limbs flail like a rag doll, twisting, crashing, down, down, down the winding stone stairwell.

One final agonizing yelp. Then silence.

XXIII.

For the briefest of moments, I pause, stunned, and numb with shock. My mind whirls with the order of events that have led me here. I look down at the hands, *my hands*, that delivered the last push. The soldier in me hesitates, but the human inside won't wait any longer.

I run down the stairs after the man, seized with worry. He might still be alive. He might still need help. My legs move rapidly downward, around and around the spiral tower stairs.

He lies near the bottom of the stairwell, crumpled in a grotesque heap, arms and legs bent in ways a body should not bend.

I crouch beside him. Slowly, cautiously, slipping my hand under the matted beard to feel for breath, a pulse, *anything*. But there is none.

His eyes are wide open, trapped in terror. Glazed yellow, unblinking. A monster frozen in time. I half expect them to flicker, to ignite again with rage. But they don't. There's nothing left. I feel the lifeless weight of his body, the limpness, the twist of his head. His neck is broken.

What have I killed? Who have I killed?

I sit back, my hand still on his body. The truth settles like a stone in my chest. Of course, it's a man. Not a demon. Not a ghost. Just a man. Broken, twisted, and mad. Sitting beside him, the smell hits me: age, filth, the coppery tang of blood on his hands, the hands that killed Dog.

Mercifully, dawn has arrived.

I stand and move slowly to the front door. I unbar it, take a deep, shuddering breath, and heave it open. It feels heavier than it did last night.

Light pours in, cascading across the ancient stone floor like a long-awaited blessing. I collapse into the same chair where young James died just a few nights ago.

Memories of other nights come flooding back, nights of paralyzing fear during the war, and all the young men who died caught in the grip of it.

I think of Sean and my parents. I think of Dog. And finally, at the end of it all, I hang my head in my hands and quietly sob.

XXIV.

Not an hour later, I hear voices outside. The banker and what looks to be a dozen townsfolk hurry down the tree-lined drive toward the open castle door.

Curiosity winning over fear, they've come to the haunted castle. When Mr. Walsh sees me sitting just inside the entryway, his tense shoulders sag with visible relief.

"You're alive," he breathes, touching my arm, as if to make sure.

"I am," I say. I can't bring myself to meet his eyes. "But he isn't." I point toward the crumpled body at the bottom of the North Tower stairs.

The crowd halts at the doorway, squinting into the shadows where I point. Commotion erupts as they cautiously step inside, examining the man.

"Oh, this old castle drove him mad," speculates one.

"No, mate," says another. "It was the haunting of the evil brother. He harms all souls who enter here."

"What does it matter which?" A plump woman I've never seen before declares. "Insane, or wicked, either way."

I answer questions, too exhausted to elaborate. I give the constable my name and my Virginia address.

He returns my gun and gives my shoulder a firm, almost fatherly pat. "Poor lad," he murmurs. "Poor wee lad."

I gather my things from the study, careful not to glance at the hearth. I will not look at Dog's blood, but I feel the weight of his absence.

I do not stay to collect my prize. I stagger out of the castle. Out of the darkness and into the sunlight.

XV.

October 31, 1945

Dear Mr. Cornell,

I hope this letter finds you well. I obtained your address from the detectives who investigated the Doomfrys Castle incident. You left in such haste; I never had the chance to thank you properly or pay you the money you rightfully earned for completing your one-night stay at the castle.

Would it be too forward to say I was quite taken with your bravery? At the time, I couldn't quite admit how worried I was. But now that the truth has come to light, I confess I spent that night on edge, fearing I might bear the guilt of sending another young man to his death. James still weighs heavily on me. You nearly broke me, I'll admit, simply by surviving.

However, I have good news to bear. After much speculation from the townsfolk, of course, dental records from nearby counties have confirmed the identity of the beastly man who attacked you. He was no ghost or demon, just a traveling salesman who vanished several years ago. A salesman! Not a tortured soul from a cursed family line, as the rumors would have it. Just a modern madman, after all this!

Still, Doomfrys keeps its secrets. Though work has finally begun on the property, the laborers continue to report strange disturbances, tools disappearing, and wolves howling unnervingly close. Perhaps there's more to the old tales of brotherly violence than we'd like to believe. I share that thought only with you.

One last thing. On your behalf, I walked the property and located the place where your loyal animal, *Dog,* rests. I thought it might bring you comfort to know I left a small pile of wildflowers and a flat stone to mark the spot. I said a few quiet words. I hope that gesture sits well with you.

Please find enclosed a cheque for 100 British pounds. It is the very least you are owed.

With sincere thanks,
Mr. E. Walsh
Property & Estate Broker
Doomfrys, Scotland

XXVI.

I've been home from Europe for a year now. When I returned to our town, my parents' house sat empty. Aunt Geraldine made sure it stayed locked up until I returned. I noticed she took a few photographs of my mother, and she mentioned the family jelly jar that supposedly belonged to some great-grandmother. She's welcome to whatever she wants.

Virginia, though still marked by the scars of the Depression and war, is slowly mending. Much has changed. Industry hums again, people are making plans, learning to look ahead through the lens of life rather than death.

I guess that's why I finally feel ready to go up into the attic. I've avoided dusty, dark corners since Doomfrys. Anything old or musty. Anything that recalls castles with rotting tapestries and drafty rooms that never sleep.

I've spent most of my time outside, in clean, open air. But ghosts, especially the ones we carry, don't disappear, unless we choose to lay them to rest. It's time to do just that.

Sean's military things were delivered a month before my parents took ill. A heavy trunk labeled *Sean Cornell* sits like a sentinel under the slanted attic roof. Finally, I intend to address his memories. To hold Sean's things and feel close to my brother, again.

But beside the trunk is a stack of other boxes. My mother's handwriting curls across the cardboard: *Calvin's high school memories,* and *College photos.*

I kneel beside them, delaying the inevitable pain of going through Sean's things. My eyes skim the labels.

Then one box stops me cold. *Family History–Scotland,* written in neat, small letters. For a long second, I can't move. Curiosity stirs beneath my ribs and presses me forward. I lift the dusty lid.

Inside are piles of old papers. Birth certificates, marriage records, and sepia-toned photographs make up the top layer.

Further down is a picture of a large town sign: *Doomfrys, Virginia. EST. 1649.* Obviously, that catches my attention. I blink. A town named Doomfrys? Just sixty or seventy miles from here? *How have I never heard of it?*

As I dig deeper, the items grow older. Letters, yellowed and fragile, written in looping, faded script. It takes effort to decipher the penmanship, let alone the language. Official documents appear as well, bylaws from the town's founding, dated in the 1600s. My eyes catch two names on a curling page: *Elizabeth and James Doomfrys.*

At the very bottom of the box lies a single large canvas, face down. My stomach drops to the basement.

I don't need to turn it over. I know what it is.

114

My hands tremble as I lift it and slowly rotate it upright. The painting is old, faded, cracked with time, and in desperate need of repair. But it's inescapable. Shrouded in mist and nestled in the lowlands, Doomfrys Castle looms, haunting as ever.

About the Author

Sarah Collins, M.S.

Stories have always come easily to Sarah Collins. They swirl in her mind during the rhythm of a long bike ride or spark from an offhand comment among friends. Even the oddest or most unsettling detail can ignite endless possibilities, fueling the imagination behind her stories.

As an author, Sarah writes across multiple genres, including pulse-quickening adventure, tender romance, gripping thrillers, and richly textured historical fiction. With a lifelong love of learning, she seeks to craft words that transport readers while connecting them to the shared threads of the human experience.

Sarah lives in the Bay Area of California with her family and pets. She loves imagining the future, visiting Yosemite, one of her happiest places, and following the next idea wherever it may lead.

Other Books by Sarah Collins

- *A Coat of Crimson or Violet*, Book I in the Pairings Duology, release date December 2025
- *Yours in Light or Darkness*, Book II in the Pairings Duology, coming soon.